THE SHERIFF'S SWEET SURRENDER

TAKE A CHANCE BOOK 6

NANCY WARREN

THE SHERIFF'S SWEET SURRENDER

He was the last man she could have, and the only one she wanted.

Welcome to Hidden Falls, Oregon where the big, crazy Chance family are finding love one by one.

Sheriff James Chance is a burned out Seattle cop who's come home to Hidden Falls where he loves his quiet life as a sheriff — quiet except for a determined divorcee who's stalking him, and the shy baker who's trying to avoid him.

Kimberly Parker left home and the shame of her past to start fresh in Hidden Falls. Little did she know that the town sheriff was the man she'd fallen for at a wedding and been avoiding ever since. Now she's working in his sister's bakery and she sees him everyday. Can she keep her secrets and her heart safe from the sexy sheriff?

CHAPTER 1

*J*ames Chance sidled up to the front door of Sunflower Coffee and Tea Company and peered inside. He figured he looked more like a burglar casing the joint than the town sheriff as he searched the busy café for trouble.

Trouble, in this case, wasn't criminals who might want to hold up the bakery in hopes of cleaning out the till, or stealing his sister Iris Chance McLeod's morning glory muffin recipe. Trouble right now, for him, meant a certain very determined divorcee, Loreen Ludlaw, who took way too personal an interest in James, to the point that stalking would not be too strong a term. He'd considered a restraining order on Loreen but nixed that idea when his brother Evan, a lawyer, told him it would make him the town laughingstock. Though he suspected the good people of Hidden Falls, Oregon were already enjoying the joke at his expense.

As his trained cop's gaze rapidly swept the inside of the coffee shop he recognized most of the customers. A table of older women laughing over their bright pottery mugs. A couple of young mothers in running gear, their babies sleeping in jogging strollers beside the table. A young man in a corner with his laptop open. He was a budding screenwriter who seemed to treat Iris's coffee shop as his office. Since Iris offered free Internet along with the best brownies ever baked, she drew a number of people who studied, worked, or played on their computers amid all the chatter and noise of a busy café.

Loreen wasn't on the premises, so he relaxed enough to open the door and walk inside. Even though he'd been expecting it, the noise still hit him—the laughter and the buzz of conversations. One of the babies began to fuss and its mother automatically reached into the stroller to pick up the crying infant. At the sound of the cheerful bells announcing his arrival, one of the older women in the coffee party glanced up and sent him a nod and a smile, which he returned.

He strode up to the counter where Iris worked the barista machine like the pro she was. Iris was pregnant with twins and from the way she was standing he suspected her back was bothering her. When she saw him, her face lit up with a smile. "Hey, little brother," she said. "What's up?"

Among his ten siblings, if he had to choose a favorite, he'd pick two: his twin brother, Josh, because they shared the unbreakable bond of twins, and Iris. Iris was the oldest girl in the family, and in many ways more nurturing than their mom. Iris had a way about her that made a person not only want to trust her, but to lay their burdens and problems on her shoulders.

She gave excellent advice, never blabbed secrets, and, unlike most of the rest of them, wasn't given to teasing. She was also about to make him an uncle for the first time. He was happy to see a new generation of Chances being born. Plus, it was cool that they were twins.

"I was in the neighborhood," he said. While he didn't walk the business area of Hidden Falls every day, he was a familiar presence. He'd discovered that community policing was more about deterring crime and encouraging neighborliness than dealing with serious law-breaking. Which made a nice change from his last job.

Iris nodded, and her smile peeped out once more. "And I'm sure my morning glory muffins had nothing to do with your sudden urge to see me."

He shook his head. "I'm always happy to see you." He shrugged, "Snarfing muffins is an added bonus." He waited as she placed a latte up on the counter and called, "Angela!" before asking, "Can I have an Americano with the muffin?"

"Coming right up. You want that to go?"

He was about to say, "No." He planned to sit inside and hopefully to get Iris to join him so he could ask her excellent advice on how to deal with the prickly issue of Loreen Ludlow, but before he could speak a woman walked out from the kitchen carrying a tray of freshly baked brownies. When he glanced up at her, the earth seemed to stop turning. The chatter behind him faded to utter silence as he stared.

She wore her long blonde hair tied back in a ponytail, her slim body was wrapped in an apron with a big yellow sunflower in the center, identical to Iris's. Beneath the apron, she wore faded jeans and sneakers that, while clean, were old and worn. Her focus had been on the tray in her hands, but as though she felt his scrutiny, she glanced up. Those big blue eyes that he remembered so well opened wide and her pale skin flushed red and then fluttered back to unnaturally pale.

Her hands tightened on the aluminum baking sheet as though she were in danger of dropping it. Since she'd come to his town, and was working for his sister, she had to have known she would see him again. And it was she who spoke first. She said, in the soft voice that haunted his dreams, "Hello, James."

He blinked and the world began to spin again. Once more he

could hear the chatter and noise behind him. "Kimberly. Hi." It was all he could manage from a suddenly dry throat. He felt foolish, thrown off his stride, and the fact that his sister was glancing between the two of them with undisguised curiosity only added to the stress of the moment.

To Iris he said, "I'll take that coffee to go."

He and Kimberly were going to have a little chat about what she was doing here, and soon. But for now he obeyed his instinct to retreat from a scene that was too hot for him to handle.

That woman, with her frail beauty, had already rocked his world once. Now that she'd come to his town, he had a bad feeling she was going to do it again.

Kimberly felt like a fool as she placed the fresh brownies into the display case, perfectly aware that her hands were trembling and that Iris was watching her intently.

Of course, in a bakery and coffee shop that was always busy, where there was barely ever a moment for her and Iris to chitchat, suddenly everyone either had full cups of coffee or were getting ready to leave. The bell wasn't ringing to announce fresh customers. Of all times, when she least wanted it, they had a lull.

When she finished with the brownies, she saw that Iris had leaned back against the counter and crossed her hands under her rounded belly in a gesture that was already growing familiar to Kimberly. "You should sit down," Kim said. "Take a break."

Iris gazed back at her with an expression that said as clearly as words, *No, I am not going to stay out of your business.* What she actually said was, "I'll take a break in a minute. How do you know my brother?"

Okay, so she wasn't going for subtle. Kim sighed. "I met him at a wedding."

Iris waited, but she had no more to say. If Iris wanted more details, let her ask James for them.

"Lots of women know my brother, and don't look as though the Headless Horseman is bearing down on them when they catch sight of him." She paused for a moment and shifted as though her back were bothering her. "It crossed my mind that maybe he'd arrested you."

The curse of her pale skin was that she blushed so easily. She also burned if she was in the sun for any length of time, but there was sunscreen for that. So far she'd never found any kind of cosmetic she could apply that would hide her blushes.

The words hung there, not an accusation, or a question, exactly, but a comment that obviously needed a reply.

"No, of course not! He's never arrested me. I've never been arrested." Her face felt hot enough to ignite her eyebrows and she sounded guilty and defensive even to her own burning ears. Would she never get away from her past?

It was, strangely enough, because of the same wedding where she'd met James that she'd been introduced to Iris. Kimberly was a trained baker who needed a change and Iris needed help in her bakery. Rose, James and Iris's sister, and one of the other brides-maids in the wedding party, had recalled Kim was a baker, and had hooked her and Iris up.

When Iris had phoned and asked if she'd be interested in working at Sunflower Coffee and Tea Company, she'd been thrilled at the opportunity to get out of Portland and live some-where quiet. Iris must have given her married name, for she hadn't made the connection with James, obviously, or she'd have turned down the opportunity right away.

It was only a couple of hours drive to Hidden Falls, Oregon but it was a world away from Portland. Smaller, with a charming main street of brick-fronted stores from the turn of the last century. She liked everything about the small town, including its name. If a waterfall could stay hidden, then why couldn't she?

Kim had also taken to Iris right away. The job interview had been more like two friends chatting over coffee. Still, during the hour or so they spent together she'd told her potential new boss about her training at the British Columbia Culinary Academy where she'd specialized in breads and pastries.

"British Columbia? Are you Canadian?" Iris asked.

"I'm a dual citizen."

"That must be nice. I drove all across Canada one summer and I thought it was beautiful."

"It is." And still she planned never to go back. Before Iris could ask anything more about her personal life, she began describing her work experience baking everything from brioche to puff pastry to gluten free bread. "I'm not afraid to work hard and I'm used to starting my shift as early as three a.m."

Iris nodded. "There's no sleeping late in our business. Even on my days off I still wake with the birds. It's an occupational hazard, I guess."

"I've never been a late sleeper." Where she'd grown up, if it wasn't a new baby crying, there were strange noises and comings and goings in the night that she had to pretend to know nothing about.

"How are you at working out front?" When Kim stared at her, she said, "With customers?"

"Oh. I'm usually in the kitchen." Obviously a small bakery/coffee shop like this wouldn't give her the luxury of staying in the kitchen all day. But it was a tiny town. Who'd ever discover her here? She could tell from Iris's expression that customer service was going to be an important part of the job. She hid the root of her hesitation by pointing toward the counter and saying, "You'd have to train me to run that fancy Barista machine. I've never used one before."

Iris sent her a relieved smile. "It's not nearly as complicated as it looks. Where do you work now?"

"I'm at a cake factory. We bake wedding cakes mostly, but also birthday, graduation, retirement, that kind of thing."

"Can I ask why you're thinking of leaving?"

How to explain the itchy feeling at the back of her neck that crept up suddenly, and caused her to pack her bags and move on. She shrugged. "Cakes are fine, but I'm getting buttercream frosting fatigue."

Iris nodded. "I'm the same. I love variety. When I first started Sunflower I was scared I'd get bored, but there's no time to be bored and I change up the menu quite a bit while keeping a staple of favorites. It seems to work." She glanced down at her belly. "As you can see, I'm expecting." She grimaced. "Twins, in fact. My plan is to hire a second baker, someone who can take over for a little while when I have the babies."

"Twins, wow. Congratulations."

Iris rubbed her belly. "Thanks. It's so much to take on. But I guess I'll figure it out, especially if I'm not worried about running the bakery at the same time as getting used to being a mom."

"I'd be happy to help in any way I can." For a moment she flashed back to saying the same words to her own mother, when she was expecting yet again. At least this time she'd be helping as a paid baker instead of an unpaid mother's helper.

Iris pushed her mug back suddenly as though she'd come to a decision. "Do you want to make something right now?"

She was a little taken aback. "Make something?"

"Sure. Best way I can think of to see if you're a fit. Let's bake a batch of muffins, or brownies, or anything you like." She rose to her feet and picked up both of their mugs in one smooth motion. "So long as I have the ingredients. My associate Dosana–" She paused. "I don't know why I said that. She's not my associate, she's my friend. Dosana started working here part-time when she was taking business school. Now she runs our second location. Anyway, she's dropping by this afternoon. It's great that she can meet you."

Kim doubted very much that Dosana's dropping by when she was here was pure coincidence but she was certain that if Iris wanted her to bake something and meet her other employee then she was seriously interested in hiring her. And Kim was seriously interested in taking the job.

Kim ran her eyes rapidly over the display case. The store was empty of customers since it was six o'clock at night and the bakery had closed. A few muffins and about half a dozen croissants were bagged up as day old merchandise to be sold off at half price in the morning. On top of the display case were jars containing cookies. The chocolate chip jar was nearly full but the one proclaiming Extra Crunchy Peanut Butter Cookies was nearly empty.

"Let's make some peanut butter cookies," she said, knowing that would be more useful to Iris than her showing off with something the bakery didn't stock.

"You're on," Iris said.

They went into the back kitchen and Kim had a chance to check out the setup and was impressed. The kitchen was well set up and orderly which would make rush times more efficient. The stainless-steel tables were topped with either butcher block or marble, perfect for pastry. There were two big, industrial mixers, two ovens and an entire wall of mixing bowls, measuring cups and tins and sheets for baking bread, cakes and cookies.

The fridge was huge, as was the dishwasher and the ingredients were all labeled, everything from flour to cardamom. There was a tiny office, a staff washroom and a back door. The walls were subway tile and the floor an industrial tile, all currently sparkling and easy to keep clean.

She was wearing a short-sleeved blue blouse, white slacks and black Nikes. She checked that her hair was well secured in its ponytail and then walked to the sink to wash her hands. When she turned, Iris handed her a large white apron with the sunflower logo on it.

As they worked, Iris showed her where things were kept and passed her ingredients. "I call the cookies extra crunchy because I use crunchy peanut butter and add in whole peanuts."

She nodded, setting the big mixer to cream the butter and sugar mixture and beginning to break eggs.

"Did you always want to be a baker?" Iris asked as she opened the stainless steel drawer labeled *flour*.

"I fell into it because it was something I could do." Her mother's voice echoed. *Kimberly, honey, I don't know what we'd do without you. You're so good in the kitchen! Mommy's little helper.*

At six she could make porridge, peel vegetables and feed and change a baby. By ten she was cooking meals and by the age of twelve she made all the bread and did most of the cooking for a large and growing family.

While the cookies were baking, Iris said, "Even though I do this every day, the smell of baking still reminds me of home. Not that my mother is the world's greatest cook. We had a big family and not much money, so there was never anything fancy in our home, but always plenty to eat and lots of laughter." She wiped down the counters while Kim cleaned the mixer. "I'm the oldest girl, so I was always helping out. Guess that's how I learned to love cooking."

Kim was amazed at how similar their backgrounds were. "How big is your family?"

Iris scrunched up her nose. "There are eleven kids."

"Eleven. Wow. We were only six, but it seemed like a hundred."

"You the oldest?"

She nodded.

A glance of understanding passed between them. She bet Iris had learned to cook when she was young, and had done more than her fair share of babysitting. She wondered if she and her siblings were close.

If she'd known how close, and that James Chance was one of

those siblings, Kim would have run out of the bakery, jumped in her car and sped away.

But she didn't know, so, when Iris pulled the industrial sized cookie sheet out of the oven, sampled the cookie before it had even finished cooling and proclaimed it 'delicious,' she'd been happy.

CHAPTER 2

*C*ould her luck get any worse? She'd finally found a place she felt safe, tucked away, untraceable, and she'd stumbled into a place where the sexiest sheriff who ever wore a badge happened to live and work.

Of course her first instinct was to pack up and hit the road now she knew that James Chance was the sheriff of Hidden Falls and the brother of her new boss, but she'd already accepted the job, given up her tiny studio apartment above a deli, where she helped out sometimes to reduce her rent, quit her minimum wage bakery job, packed her bags and driven here in her battered old Ford.

Iris had never suggested any kind of a criminal check and Kim was pretty sure she hadn't done one. Instead, she'd asked Kim to come back for a second interview later the same evening when she'd met both Geoff, Iris's husband, and Dosana, her only other full-time employee, who ran a second Sunflower bakery in a nearby town.

The not-quite question hung in the air and Kim knew that, as friendly as Iris was, she expected an explanation for her strange behavior in front of the town sheriff. She took the tray back into the kitchen to give herself a moment and when she returned she offered one truth, while hiding another. "Please don't tell James this, but when I met him, I kind of fell for him. It was at a wedding where I was a bridesmaid and you know how weddings always make you act a little crazy? I guess that's why I was embarrassed to see him again."

Iris nodded. "I may be his sister, but I can see that James is super hot." The line of worry that had formed on Iris's brow didn't completely disappear, however. Kim understood her feelings. Iris had been honest with her newest employee that it had been very hard to find someone who had both bakery experience and a willingness to relocate to Hidden Falls. Maybe now she was beginning to think that her luck had been too good to be true. Kim couldn't blame her.

She escaped as soon as she could from that worried gaze and went out front to bus tables. Two women with babies and jogging strollers were preparing to leave. One woman held a crying infant in one arm and was attempting to put her jacket on with the other while her friend was already halfway to the door with her own stroller. Kim dropped her cleaning rag on the table and in her quiet voice said, "What a beautiful baby. Could I hold her for a second?"

The young mother looked insanely grateful as she nodded and Kim reached for the tiny, squalling, red-faced baby. She held the little squirming body against her shoulder, rocking her own body and whispering soothing nonsense. The baby quieted almost immediately and the mom heaved a sigh of relief as she put her jacket on and rapidly packed up the baby paraphernalia that littered the table and tucked it away in the baby stroller. She gazed at Kim in amazement. "You are really good with babies."

Kim smiled, handing back the now-quiet child. "I like babies. I think they can sense it. Have a great day."

The women left and she went back to bussing tables. She walked past an older gentleman who was working a crossword puzzle. When he reached for his coffee he absently elbowed his pencil onto the floor. She barely broke stride, bending to pick up the pencil and replacing it at his side.

She and Iris worked together efficiently, though she was aware that her new boss was still wondering about her extreme reaction to seeing James again. Speaking of extreme reactions, Kim couldn't stop picturing the night of the wedding. Her and James…

When things grew quiet, Iris said, "I think I'm going to head out for an hour or so and try to get some rest. Are you okay for a while?"

Kim nodded.

"Call me if it gets busy or you need anything."

"I will." After Iris left, she went into the back for her purse and got her cell phone. There was a phone call she needed to make.

After several rings, a familiar voice answered. "Hello?"

She stood with her body partly in the kitchen and partly out front, so she could keep an eye on the tables and said softly, "Hey, Mom, it's me."

"Kimberly. How are you, baby?" She smiled at the word. She hadn't been a baby for a long time. In fact, since she was about six years old and there were too many other babies. In the background she could hear one of them wailing even now.

"I'm fine. How are you?"

Her mom sighed. "Bitty's teething and little Kenny's got croup." Her mom lowered her voice. "I'm so tired. All the time."

She bit her lip, picturing the old kitchen where her mom spent most of her time. It was dilapidated and messy, and even though she knew she could never fix what was wrong, she still felt the urge to try. Then a new voice bellowed in the background. "Who's that on the phone?"

"It's Kimberly, Honey."

He didn't take the phone, just bellowed louder. "Margie's got her hands full, we could sure use your help around the place."

She closed her eyes against a wash of weakness. He'd gone straight to the one thing he knew might bring her back. "Do you really need me, Mom?"

There was a pause and she imagined her father had gone out again, then her mom said, "No. I don't want you back here. You got out and I wish to hell I could. If you can get settled then maybe when your brothers and sisters get older you can help them. It's all that keeps me going, some days."

"Okay." She was so relieved. She never wanted to go back. Never. "Mom, I've got a new job." Briefly, she told her mother about the bakery.

"That's great, Kim."

"Look, I could send you a little money if you need it."

Her mom laughed, and even her laugh sounded tired. "Money's the one thing we aren't short of."

She sighed. "Until Daddy ends up in jail."

Her mom's tone sharpened in an instant. "You know our family rule. Loyalty at all costs. Don't you even think about turning your dad over to the cops. Think what would happen to the rest of us. The little ones would get taken away and put in foster care." Her mom's voice rose in panic. "Please."

She closed her eyes against the rush of helpless frustration. "I would never do that. I promise. No cops."

Which meant that James Chance was the one man she could never have, no matter how much she wanted him. Keeping family secrets could sure be tough on a girl.

She turned to glance one more time at the café before returning her cell phone to her purse and only then noticed an older woman standing beside the cash register. She'd been just outside of Kim's peripheral vision.

How much had she heard?

∼

"THERE'S A WOMAN TO SEE YOU." Connie's bored voice over the intercom caused James to jerk like he'd been jump-started. He was on his feet so fast he had to take a breath to slow himself down. Ever since he'd seen Kimberly that morning, he'd been unable to get her out of his mind. He stood, schooling his face to impassive, reminding himself that he couldn't kiss the woman senseless when she first walked in no matter how much he wanted to.

"Thanks. Send her in." But when Connie ushered the woman in to see him, his interest drained. It wasn't Kimberly standing in front of him, her long hair like golden light, her nervous eyes darting to his and away again. It was Edna May Tittlebury.

Edna May was a stalwart citizen of Hidden Falls and the biggest old busybody in Oregon as far as James could tell. He didn't sit back down, hoping a standing conversation would mean a shorter one. "Edna May," he said, trying not to sound disappointed. "What can I do for you?"

Her eyes were as beady and bright as a crow's and the way she pecked at news and gossip kind of reminded him of a nuisance bird, too. "I don't like to bring trouble," she said, when as far as he could tell she liked nothing more, "but I overheard something in the coffee shop I think I should report. As a good citizen."

He grabbed a notepad, as he did whenever she came in to complain about everything from kids on skateboards to the smell of marijuana in the woods near the high school. The woman could work part-time as a drug hound so acute was her sense of smell.

"Uh-ha," he said, clicking open his ballpoint pen.

"It's about that new girl in the bakery. The blonde one."

Immediately, his interest grew sharp but he kept a bland expression on his face. "What about her?"

"Iris is too trusting, that's what. What do we even know about this girl? She blows in like a tumbleweed and next thing, Iris goes out and leaves her in charge of the bakery. Why, she could clean out the till and be gone in minutes."

And why was any of that Edna May's business, he wondered silently. Aloud, he said, "Do you know something about Iris's new hire that you'd like to share?"

She pursed her lips and leaned in, looking more like a buzzard, he decided, than a crow. "I overheard that girl on the phone. She had her back to the café and was keeping her voice low, but I heard every word. I have excellent hearing." *A real bonus in a backbiting gossip.*

"What did you hear?" In spite of himself, his interest sharpened. Where Kimberly was concerned there were too many questions.

"She said, 'Okay, I promise. No cops.' That is word for word what I heard. I even wrote it down the second I got out of there so I wouldn't forget. She held up a journal type notebook with pansies painted on the front, and flipped it open to where she'd penned the words in neat handwriting. "Why would a girl be whispering about no cops if she doesn't have anything to hide? And when she turned around and saw me standing there, I swear she blushed and looked guilty as sin."

He nodded. Part of small town policing was making people feel heard, as well as safe. He figured for all the times he acted like the useless information people passed on to him was important, there'd be one time that somebody actually had something vital to share. So far it hadn't happened. "There could be a lot of explanations behind those words," he said soothingly. "I hope you won't make Hidden Falls an unfriendly place for Iris's new baker. Iris really needs the help with the twins coming."

She looked as though he'd smacked her beak. "I would never stoop to gossip." And in fall leaves would never turn color. "But I want Iris and her new family to be safe."

"I understand that, Edna May, and I'm going to look into what you've told me, in strictest confidence, of course. I want my sister to be safe just as much as you do." Then he smiled and moved toward the door, sweeping her forward with every step.

She seemed reluctant to go. She had that pansy-fronted notebook open as though she were going to share more from her journal of bitching. Then inspiration struck. What Edna May needed was a project. Something positive she could do in the community instead of making trouble. He said, "I'm so glad you stopped by. I was going to ask for your help in something."

"Policing?" She sounded far too eager. Like she thought he might offer her a deputy position, God forbid.

"No. I need some volunteers on the Fourth of July Committee." And why the sheriff of the town had to organize a Fourth of July event evaded him, but his predecessor had done it and the sheriff before that so it was pretty much written in the town bylaws that he had to run the biggest party in the Hidden Falls social calendar.

She looked crestfallen. "But I already volunteer with the church and the historical society."

"I know, and we all appreciate it, but I need some committee members that I can trust, who have experience in this town. I'm not naming names, Edna May, but there are a few volunteers who want to bring in new ideas. Who maybe think our celebration isn't exciting enough."

He might as well have flipped a switch, so fast did her face twist in outrage. "That's absolutely ridiculous. We've run the Fourth of July celebration exactly the same way every year since I was a little girl." Probably since the dinosaurs were baby lizards. "Doing things the same way is the whole point of tradition."

"I couldn't agree more. But there are always people who want to change things."

She nodded, firmly. Opened her notebook to a fresh page. "When's the next meeting? I'll be there."

"I really appreciate it. We meet in the library, next door. Connie has the details." And then he opened his office door and walked out front, so Edna May had no choice but to follow. "Connie, great news. Edna May has agreed to serve on the Fourth of July committee. Can you fill her in on the details?"

Connie looked at him like he might have lost his mind. Probably, by the time he was halfway through the next committee meeting, he'd agree with her. But the good thing about Edna May was that she had a lot of time, a lot of energy, and she did know how things had been done around here long before he was born.

He returned to his office and sat. He'd distracted Edna May but the conversation she'd overheard worried him. Why was Kim having whispered phone calls that specifically mentioned 'no cops'?

"Everybody lies," his partner, Vince, had been fond of saying. "You have to figure out what they're lying about."

Vince was dead now, shot by a notorious drug dealer in a bust gone wrong. James had killed the man who'd taken down his partner and friend, but that wouldn't bring back the guy who'd loved old horror movies and refused to believe that sushi was an edible food. As Vince had lay dying in the rain, while James listened to the ambulance siren getting closer, telling his friend to hang on even as they'd both known it would be too late, Vince had said to him, "Sometimes, life sucks." As final words went, maybe they weren't the most profound, but they'd been as true as any sentiment.

Sometimes life really did suck. James had gone on with his job, but he couldn't sleep, was twitchy and angry. "Survivor's guilt," the department psych had diagnosed him. "It's the part of PTSD that can be toughest to overcome."

He'd felt burned out, used up. He hated going to work, hated walking past Vince's locker, which stayed empty, partly out of respect and partly because nobody else wanted it. Like it might harbor bad luck. After a year of feeling like he was going to burst out of his skin, working obsessive hours, sleeping with bad dreams or not at all, he'd realized he needed a change or he'd end up dead too.

The sheriff's position in Hidden Falls had come up and he'd thought, why not? He was much younger and far better qualified than any other candidate, plus he knew the town and the area since he'd grown up there. In Hidden Falls he'd been able to function closer to normal, and he'd started to sleep again. To believe in the basic goodness of people.

And then Kimberly had come along.

He wasn't going to lie to himself. She'd rocked his world just as he'd begun to feel grounded again. And it was a world he'd quite liked steady. Even. Predictable.

The intercom went again. "There's a woman to see you," Connie announced.

Fool me once. "The same one?"

"No. A different one."

"Okay. Send her in." He was glad Kim had come to him. It meant, among other things, that she wanted to see him again. At least he hoped so. Maybe she'd come to tell him whatever it was Edna May had overheard her whispering about. He sat up straighter in his chair and tried to look like a man who was busy doing an important job, not a dude with a crush.

The door opened, and once more his hopes were dashed. "Loreen!" And of all the people he did not want to see, her name topped the list. "What can I do for you?" Then, as she smiled suggestively, he rose to his feet. "No, don't shut the door. It's fine open."

"Suit yourself." Loreen was about eight years older than he was and a good-looking woman. She was wearing a short jean skirt that showed off long, tanned legs, a white sleeveless shirt that displayed her impressive cleavage, and little silver sandals. Her hair was a smooth curtain of brown with subtle stripes of gold and copper that he bet cost a fortune and wasn't offered by The Village Coiffure here in Hidden Falls.

In fact, she was as out of place in Hidden Falls as a Vegas showgirl in a nunnery. According to his mother, who got the story from her yoga group where Loreen was a member, Loreen had been working as a low level admin in a Seattle investment firm when she met Joe Ludlow. Joe was a flashy and successful advisor who swept Loreen off her feet and soon they were married. He'd left the investment firm to start his own company and that's when things started to go south. He may have been a good salesman but he was a terrible businessman. By the time they'd moved to Hidden Falls, where real estate prices were a fraction of those in Seattle, he had few clients left. Soon, he packed up and left Loreen for one of those clients, a software developer who moved Joe back to Seattle and into her penthouse overlooking Lake Union.

In the ensuing bitter divorce, Loreen got the house in Hidden Falls and enough alimony to ensure she didn't have to work, but, presumably not enough to allow her to leave this small town. James pitied her, though he thought she should find a better way to spend her time than stalking him.

He wasn't rich or particularly ambitious, not Loreen's type at all, but he suspected that she needed to snare him, at least temporarily, to massage her wounded ego. But he wasn't an ego masseur and he wished there were more single men in the area for her to focus on.

As she sank gracefully into the visitor's chair in front of his desk and crossed her legs, he noticed that her toenails were painted dark pink and that a silver toe ring glinted. "I think I have a Peeping Tom," she said, shifting so that her skirt rode up even higher.

He jerked his gaze up to her face, annoyed that her obvious wiles were working even a tiny bit. "A Peeping Tom?" He went through a quick spin of the troublemakers in the area and couldn't imagine who, in this small town, might be the culprit. He grabbed a notebook. "Have you seen him?"

"No, but I've heard him. At night. It's really scaring me." She dropped her chin and glanced up at him through her lashes. "When I'm taking off my clothes, getting ready to slip into bed naked, he makes these noises outside my window. I was thinking maybe you could come over tonight and do a stakeout."

Oh, he didn't think so.

"Have you actually seen this guy?"

"Not exactly, but I saw a shadow. I'm sure it was a pervert running away from my house."

"When was this?"

"Last night."

He recalled that it had been windy the previous evening. He suspected she'd seen nothing but swaying tree branches and the rustling she'd heard was likely a trash can knocked over by the wind, or a prowling animal. However, he took his job seriously even if some of his constituents had nothing better to do than waste his time.

"I'll send a deputy to do a drive-by tonight and tomorrow. In the meantime, keep your curtains and blinds shut."

She pouted prettily. "Won't you come by yourself?"

She'd been pulling stunts like this for weeks and he was running out of patience. "No."

"But I get so lonely at night." Suddenly the mask fell and he saw the sadness in her. He couldn't help the reluctant sympathy he felt. "I'll put my best man on it." He had one deputy, a cheerful, chubby guy who'd never make it on a real force. What she needed was something useful to do. A project. Not even believing he was about to do what he was about to do, he said, "I'm glad you came in today. I want your help with something."

She brightened and flicked her hair behind her ear. "You do?"

"Yeah. I'm heading the committee for the Fourth of July celebration. Frankly, it's the same old, same old every year. I was wondering if you'd consider being on it? We need some new blood, some new ideas."

She didn't look thrilled at his suggestion. "What would I have to do?"

"Come to the meetings and offer suggestions. Hopefully you'll take an active role on the big day."

"And you chair these meetings?"

He hoped he wasn't doing a very stupid thing. "I do."

She looked doubtful, but shrugged. "It's not like I have anything else to do. I started working part-time for the cable TV station, but that's not very busy. Sure. I guess."

He rose and said, "That's the spirit. Connie will give you the details." Then he strode around his desk, way around, giving Loreen as much berth as he'd give a rabid skunk, and strode out to the front, once more giving Connie the good news. Connie wasn't one for drama, but her eyes widened and then she said, "Sure. One more for the Fourth of July Committee."

CHAPTER 3

*H*e waited until Loreen was gone, peering through his office blinds until he saw her drive out of the parking lot before he headed out once more to where Connie sat. He stood over her. "Okay, what is it?"

She glanced up from her computer. "Huh?"

He put his hands on his hips. *"'There's a woman to see you?'* You know every single person in this town and you know for damn sure that I'd want some warning before seeing Edna May Tittlebury or Loreen Ludlow. I assume, if you say, 'There's a woman to see you,' that the woman is a stranger to you. You're punishing me. Why?"

She sniffed. Pointed balefully at the calendar. "You know what day this is?"

Of course he knew what day it was. It was May 15th. He thought hard. It wasn't Secretary's Day was it? Did anyone even celebrate that anymore? And even if they did, was Connie a secretary? He suspected she'd be offended at the notion. Unless there was a raise involved.

His detective's gaze searched the area for clues, but there were none. She kept her space as clean as a surgeon's operating table.

Connie wasn't one for personal memorabilia. "Is it your birth-day?" he tried.

She huffed. "Of course it's my birthday. Last chief always remembered. He'd bring in a cake that his wife baked." She glared. "That woman can cook. She knew I liked chocolate and she'd bake me a chocolate cake. Every year."

He wasn't married and he certainly didn't have time to run home and bake a cake but he could see that if he wanted the office to run with any kind of efficiency today he was going to have to come up with something. Besides, he liked Connie. "I'm really sorry. I didn't know. How bout I take you out for lunch?"

Her sour expression didn't sweeten the tiniest bit. "My husband's taking me out for lunch. I'll need an extra quarter hour."

"Of course, sure." Then he thought for a moment. "Maybe you could make me a list of birthdays and help me remember them."

She seemed slightly mollified. "Okay."

He went back into his office and shut the door, then he grabbed the phone and called the only woman who could save this day for him, Iris.

He heard the coffee shop phone ring, and then a soft, breathy voice that was not his sister's answered, "Sunflower Coffee and Tea Company." Even her voice made him think of things he shouldn't, brought back memories of a night he'd never forget. He said, "Kim, it's James. Is Iris there?"

"Um, no. She went home to rest."

"Oh." Now what?

"Can I give her a message?"

"Maybe you can help me. I've got a problem." Briefly, he explained his dilemma. "I know you don't do birthday cakes, but I'm wondering if you could maybe write Happy Birthday on a brownie? Connie said she likes chocolate. I'll pick it up around one-thirty?"

"Of course. Um, do you have a birthday card to go with it?"

"Birthday card?" Next somebody was going to ask him to dress up as a clown and twist balloons into animals.

"One that everybody signs. People really seem to like those."

"Okay. I'm on it." He paused, picturing her holding the phone, wondering if she had thought of him as often as he'd thought of her and then realizing that of course she hadn't. Otherwise, she might have taken one of his calls. "Thanks."

KIM STOOD UNCERTAINLY for a moment after James's call and then, with a tiny nod, went to work. Her employment at any number of bakeries had taught her the importance of celebrating birthdays. Between serving customers out front and keeping the display case stocked, she measured sugar and butter into the big mixer, then the eggs, added flour, a generous measure of the good cocoa Iris used.

When Iris returned, she suffered a qualm of nervousness. What if she'd overstepped the bounds? Maybe she should have asked Iris before she started that cake.

"How are things?" Iris asked, wrapping the apron around her. Without thinking, Kim stepped forward and tied the tapes for her. "Thanks."

"You're welcome. Everything's fine. Um, I've done something. I hope you don't mind."

"Would it have anything to do with the heavenly smell of chocolate coming from the kitchen?"

She nodded. Briefly explained James's dilemma. "I probably should have asked you first, but I was in a rush to get the cake ready by one-thirty. I'm sorry."

Iris put an arm around her shoulder and squeezed. "Don't be sorry. You did great. It makes me really happy to know that you have good instincts. It's one cake. James will be thrilled and let me tell you, it's never a good thing to have Connie on your bad side. That woman has a mean streak a mile wide." Then she grabbed for the phone. "I'd better call James and tell him to buy a card and have everyone sign it. He'll never think of it himself."

"Actually, I did suggest that, when he was on the phone."

"That man owes you big."

She would not blush, she wouldn't... Damn! She felt the heat slide up her face and turned away so Iris wouldn't see. Though Iris could probably feel the heat coming off her. "I'd better go and check on the cake."

The cake was perfectly cooked so she took the pans out to cool and when she returned out front, Iris was chatting to a very pretty middle-aged woman. She turned and said, "It's your lucky day. You got to see my brother, now you get to meet my mom. Daphne, this is Kim, who probably saved James's life today."

"No, I didn't."

Daphne shook her hand heartily. "It's a pleasure to meet you. Iris really needs the help."

"Mom, you make me sound like I'm incompetent."

"Not incompetent, darling, just very pregnant and over-worked." She shook her head. "What were you thinking, having twins your first time out?"

"I didn't exactly plan it."

"I didn't plan James and Josh, either, but somehow we got through it. 'Course, that wasn't my first rodeo. I already had what, half a dozen of you little ones? What were two more?"

Her casual attitude fascinated Kim. In fact, everything about James and Iris's mom fascinated her. She thought of her own mother, worn down from kids and worry and living with her dad. She looked old enough to be Daphne's mother and she'd had a lot fewer kids.

As though reading her mind, Daphne said, "I didn't give birth to them all, of course. Some were gifted to me. I've been blessed by every one of my children."

Iris piped up, "And before you ask, we have a family rule that no one ever tells which are Daphne and Jack's kids by birth and which are adopted."

Kim heartily approved. "So you treat them all the same."

Daphne had eyes like sea glass, both green and blue at the same time. "That's right. Every child should feel loved and wanted."

"I would have loved to have a mother like you," she blurted. Then rushed to say, "Not that my mom didn't do her best, but, well…"

"I think every mother does her best. But it doesn't come easy to all of us. Kids have to be very forgiving."

"That's a good way to put it."

Daphne turned to Iris. "So, have you heard the news?"

"What news?"

"That your brother's completely lost his mind?"

"If you're talking about Prescott, he was born crazy."

"Not Prescott, and really, I think the term for Scott is eccentric genius." She turned to Kim who was standing there mystified. "Prescott Chance is one of my kids."

"Prescott Chance the famous architect is your brother?"

"And eccentric genius," Iris added.

"Stop changing the subject. I'm not talking about Prescott, I'm talking about James!"

Kim's attention sharpened. Iris said, "I'd have said he was one of the sanest of the Chances, not that that's saying much. What's he gone and done? Given you a speeding ticket?"

Daphne chuckled. "He tried to once. Told him I'd call up the local paper and tell embarrassing stories from when he was a kid. He let me off with a warning." She turned to Kim, "I can tell you a few of those stories if you like, in case you're ever in trouble with the law."

It was said jokingly but once more she felt heat suffuse her cheeks. She wondered if there was an operation she could have that would stop her giveaway blushes. She shook her head and said, "I don't want to know his embarrassing secrets. Thanks anyway." And she certainly didn't want him or his family to know hers.

"Suit yourself. Offer stays open."

Iris passed her mom a chai latte and said, "So, how has James lost his mind?"

"He's asked Edna May Tittlebury to sit on his Fourth of July committee."

"Really? Doesn't he know that she's a trouble-making gossip?"

"There's more. He invited Loreen Ludlow to be on the same committee." Daphne sipped from her drink with an air of satisfaction as her daughter stared, dumbfounded.

Finally, Iris said, "No. Not possible. Somebody's messing with you."

"If somebody is, it would your brother. James told me so himself."

"But he skulks around town trying to *avoid* Loreen Ludlow. You should see him peering in the window before he comes into the bakery, just in case she's in here. Why would he ask her to sit on a committee that he chairs?"

"He says she needs something to do with her time."

"We all know what she wants to do with her time, and it involves getting hot and steamy with my brother the sheriff."

Kim felt an irrational and unwanted spurt of jealousy. She wanted to be the one getting hot and steamy with the sheriff. Except she didn't. That was a terrible idea and she resolutely put it out of her mind.

"He told me that he's hoping if she gets involved in the committee that she'll stop stalking him."

"Do you think it will work?" Kim asked, sounding doubtful.

"No. I don't. And I told him so."

"Then what did he say?"

"Then he conned me into going on his Fourth of July committee to protect him from Loreen."

Iris started to laugh. "This is one committee that could actually be fun. Oh, my. I'd love to be a fly on the wall at those meetings."

Daphne laughed a slightly sinister laugh. "Why don't you volunteer to provide refreshments? That way you can watch the show without having to do any organizing."

"If I wasn't seventy-five months pregnant, I would."

"Try to rest as much as you can, darling." Daphne picked up her drink and then said, "Oh, I forgot to tell you that Marguerite and Alexei are back from their trip to Greece. They're coming for dinner Sunday. You in?"

"Of course," Iris said.

"And Kim, I'd love it if you could come too."

"Oh. I hadn't... I mean..." She glanced at Iris and down at the counter uncertain what to say. She wasn't normally invited to socialize with her employers. But she was beginning to realize that Iris wasn't like anyone she'd ever worked for, and her family, the few of them she'd met, certainly weren't like any family she'd ever known.

"Don't let Mom push you into anything you don't want to do, but I promise the food will be good and my family is impossible to describe but something you have to experience."

"Well, thank you. I'd love to come. What can I bring?"

"Bring yourself. And a sense of humor. You'll need it to get through one of our dinners. Now I'll stop bothering you two and go sit with my friends." And she moved to one of the window tables where she was soon deep in conversation with a couple of other women who came in regularly.

Iris turned to her. "You don't have to come if you don't want to, you know. Mom's mission in life is to keep expanding her family."

"I like your mom."

"You have good taste. Everyone does, but she can carry you away with her enthusiasm sometimes."

"I'll remember that."

Kim loved the soothing action of icing a cake, swishing the frosting until it was smooth, then piping a pattern around the edges. She got the feeling that Connie was a traditional woman so she used a rich pink icing to make roses, and white for the ribbon and finally a deep green for the leaves. She wrote the script in careful white. *Happy Birthday Connie.* And she was done.

She was easing the cake into a box when Iris came into the back and immediately peeked. "Oh, that is so pretty. I wish it was my birthday."

She smiled at the mildly petulant tone of a constantly hungry pregnant woman. "When it's your birthday I'll make you an even nicer cake."

"I can't wait." Then Iris sighed. "We have an emergency."

"We do?" She didn't smell smoke, see water pooling anywhere or hear screaming, and Iris didn't look like a woman near panic, so she took her time getting worked up. "What's the emergency?"

"James claims he was standing in the stationary store looking at cards when he got called out. He's begging us to help him. He needs a card and Ralph at the stationary store told him they always used to get balloons for Connie's birthday, so he wonders if one of us could get the card and balloons and drop everything off at the station?"

"Oh."

"I was wondering if that someone could be you?"

"Me? Go to the police station?" She'd rather stand naked on the North Pole. With Santa and the reindeer watching.

"Is that a problem?" Iris sounded concerned.

She had to get a grip. "No. It's fine. I'll be fine." And she hoped that would be true.

She found, when she got to the stationary store, that Ralph, the guy who ran it, was inclined to be chatty. He showed her the cards, gave his opinion on every one of them, and when she chose, "From all of us on your birthday," told her, "That's the same card they got her last year."

Finally, she asked, "Which one do you suggest?"

He confided that he had a new selection of cards and that he thought Connie would like the one featuring a bunch of cartoon animals. He'd already blown up the helium balloons, so all she had to do was pay for the few items, load them in her car with the cake, and head the short distance to the sheriff's office.

As she pulled into the civic lot shared with the library, her dad's voice echoed in her ear. "Stay away from cops, girl. They bring nothing but trouble."

Still, she forced herself to remain calm as she approached City Hall. She hauled the birthday supplies out, then realized she'd give away how little James had actually done if she marched into the main door with the cake and the balloons. She hesitated, and then saw a chubby man in a uniform getting out of a squad car and heading into the building.

"Excuse me," she said, "could you tell me where the Sheriff is?"

He looked for a moment like a Jeopardy contestant sweating over the final answer, before he said, "Should be inside." He gestured to the door that said Sheriff's Office. She'd felt her familiar dread when she'd seen his uniform but now, given his vacuous expression and the overheated redness of his face, she began to feel more in control. She said, "I have a cake and balloons for Connie's birthday. I don't want her to see me bringing them in. Is there a way we can get them in without going past her?"

"Oh, yeah. Good point. It's her birthday today. She was not happy when she thought we'd forgotten."

"But you didn't forget," she said patiently. "The sheriff ordered the cake and things. All we have to do is get them inside without Connie seeing them. Then you can surprise her."

He paused for a moment, thinking, then said, "I'll sneak you in the back way."

"Excellent." So, she followed the uniformed deputy around the side of the building to a back door. "I'll make sure the coast is clear," he said in a stage whisper, then entered. A moment later he was back and beckoning her inside.

She could feel unease prickle up her backbone, but she tried to stay calm as she followed him inside and down a corridor, a turn and then through a doorway. She'd assumed they were going to a staff room or something, so stopped dead in surprise when she found herself confronting James for the second time that day. "Hey, Sheriff, someone to see you," the deputy said, before backing out of the room again.

"Hi," she said.

James rose from behind a computer screen and his smile was warm as he stepped forward. "You are a lifesaver. Iris said you made a cake specially, and I see you picked up the card and balloons. I don't know how to thank you."

"It's nothing," she mumbled. Placing the cake box on his desk, along with the card and then handing him the balloon bouquet.

She turned to leave but he stopped her saying, "Kim. We need to talk."

What could she say to him? She couldn't tell him the truth and she didn't want to lie. There was so much she wanted to say to him and so little that she could share. She said, "I know. But not right now. I've got to get back to the bakery. Another time."

And then she left quickly, as though her life depended on getting away.

CHAPTER 4

"*We have to talk?*" That was the smooth line James had come up with? Using the world's corniest line was bad enough, but he'd done it while holding a fistful of pink and silver balloons wafting above his head.

She'd all but run out the door and he'd let her go. He didn't want her to think of him the way he thought of Loreen Ludlow.

He wanted to call her and tell her that Connie had loved the cake and staff-sheriff morale was at an all time high. But he didn't. He didn't even drop by for his morning Americano.

Before he saw Kim again, he was hoping to get a few minutes alone with Iris to ask for her advice when they met up at his parents' place for a barbecue.

As James walked into the ramshackle Chance residence he found the usual Sunday night chaos. Too many people trying to talk over each other, the dog barking and wagging her tail to show she wanted in the conversation, too.

He didn't knock. No one did. He walked in, headed to the kitchen where his mom was hefting an enormous colander filled with strawberries to the sink. He lifted the colander out of her hands. "Thanks, honey," she said, turning on the tap so he could rinse the berries.

That done, she told him to head out back. "Dad's barbecuing burgers. He strode out the back door, grabbed a cold beer from the cooler, and headed for the gathered crowd. It occurred to him that the Chance clan was growing and the house wasn't. He sidled up to Prescott, his architect brother, who was down for the weekend with his fiancé, Holly. "When are you going to design a house we can all fit in?"

Behind his Ray-Bans, his brother closed his eyes as though he were in pain. "Do you have any idea how much it kills me to see this place? Know that any enterprising style editor who wants to trace my beginnings can come down and see this rabbit warren and think I'm too much of a cheap ass to build my folks a decent house?"

"And are you?" He knew Scott was generous, but it was in his nature to tease. Especially where family was concerned. "A cheap ass?"

"I've offered to build them a new house. No dice. Even drawn up plans to renovate this one. They both say they love the place as it is and their tie is sentimental." He gazed around the worn wooden siding, the sagging porch their dad had built, and through the big window they could see inside the main living area where the wear and tear of nearly a dozen kids had taken its toll. "Sentimental? The place is a dump."

But when he thought of a Prescott Chance designed masterpiece sitting in place of this overgrown cottage, he saw his parents' point. Sure, it was cramped and noisy, but it was home.

Before he could provoke an argument, Holly walked up with her friendly smile. He'd liked her from the first second she walked into their home, uninvited, desperate to get the famous architect to design a home for her asshat of a boss. She'd done it, too, by virtue of determination, friendliness in the face of Scott's icy reserve, and the unsubtle efforts of the entire family to interfere.

He'd had a bit of a crush on her, more so when he realized Scott did, too, and then the natural sibling rivalry kicked in, but he'd never had a hope. The woman with the wild corkscrew hair and winning smile was the polar opposite of his orderly brother and somehow his exact match.

"James, Hi. It's so good to see you," she said, holding her arms wide for a hug. "You have to come to San Francisco and visit us soon. Doesn't he, Prescott?"

His brother made a sound that was open to interpretation. He grinned and said, "Scott doesn't want me visiting, he knows I'll sweep you off your feet and run away with you."

She appeared delighted with the idea. "You are so good for my ego." And she kissed him on the cheek. Since all of them knew that was never going to happen, Prescott didn't even summon the energy to threaten to take him apart. Clearly, they were finally growing up.

Scott wore black linen pants that somehow held their crease, and a white short-sleeved shirt tucked in with symmetrical precision. Holly, on the other hand, wore a flowered skirt, with a bright yellow top that had already come untucked on one side. She had sandals on her feet and hadn't completely buckled one of them as though she'd been in too much of a hurry to finish getting ready. Knowing Holly she'd been doing three things at once.

Even when she was perfectly put together she still managed to look disheveled. She was like this house, a little messy but that was part of her charm. They all loved her, not only for herself, but because she'd made Prescott closer to human.

He felt arms wrap around his waist from behind and turned to find his sister Lauren. "LouLou," he said, using the baby name he'd given her when she arrived in their family and he was two. "It's great to see you. When did you get into town?" Lauren was a recently qualified vet who worked for a family practice doing everything from birthing cows to spaying kittens. Since she was the newest vet in the practice, and still proving herself, she was also one of the busiest, so they didn't see her as much as he'd like.

"This afternoon. I didn't want to miss the first barbecue of the summer."

The noise level increased when the returning Greek travelers arrived. Alexei and Marguerite had become engaged in the backyard of this very home, when Iris and Geoff got married. Alex had taken his bride-to-be to his Greek homeland to meet his extended family, and, in a move that seemed like something the Chances would do, the entire US contingent of Vasilopouloses had tagged along too. That meant his sister Rose and her fiancé Matt were also looking tanned and rested after a Greek vacation.

There was much hugging and back patting, since they hadn't seen the travelers for three entire weeks. They could have been gone for years so joyful was the reunion.

The brothers came in speaking Greek. "In English!" Rose yelled, smacking Matt on the shoulder. She caught James staring and said, "They do this. Talk in Greek so we won't understand."

"Only congratulating my brother on having one of the two hottest babes this side of the Peloponnese," he said.

He didn't hear Rose's reply, no doubt a stinging one, because new arrivals crowded in and for a moment his world tilted. Iris and Geoff stepped out from the kitchen, which left his world perfectly normal, and then he noticed they'd brought Kimberly with them and that's when the globe angled. When would this stop happening to him? And, more to the point, why hadn't his mother told him she'd invited Iris's new hire to dinner?

Lauren headed toward the new arrivals, but he stood rooted to the spot.

As though she felt his gaze on her, Kim glanced around and caught his eye. He resisted the urge to stride up to her, his recent *we need to talk* embarrassment, complete with balloons, making him hold back.

To his surprise, instead of blushing and trying to get away like she usually did when he was around, she moved around behind Iris, who was busy showing off to her sisters how much her belly had grown in three weeks, and came toward him. "Hi," she said, shy but friendly. "How was the birthday party?"

Okay. Friendly. He could do that. "We pulled it off, thanks to you. And I have to say that is one of the best chocolate cakes I've ever eaten." He leaned closer, "Don't let my mom hear, but the best, in fact."

She ignored his compliment on her cake-baking skills and asked, "So, Connie's forgiven you?"

"She has. Until the next time I screw up, which won't be long."

Her eyes twinkled. They weren't a deep, striking blue, more the soft blue of a periwinkle. "Do you screw up a lot?"

He shifted from one foot to the other. How to explain? "See, I learned policing in a bigger town. I solved murders and busted drug rings. I didn't have to buy birthday balloons and oversee dog licenses. So, yeah, I screw up." He hadn't missed the way her expression had clouded for a second when he'd mentioned drug busts. The niggle in his gut that had been there, like a squirming tadpole right behind his belly button, since she moved to town, grew more intense. He said, "But I guess you know what it's like, moving from a bigger city to this backwater."

"Baking is pretty much baking, wherever you do it."

Then his mother swooped down. "Kim, I'm so happy you came." That was the great thing about his mother. She made every lost soul feel at home. And he had a feeling that Kim was definitely lost.

"It's nice of you to have me. Oh, here," and she presented a paper bag. "These are a Canadian specialty."

"Whereabouts in Canada is home?" he asked, hoping he sounded casual.

"Oh, a small town you'd never have heard of." And before he could press, his mother was exclaiming over the contents of the bag. "You are such a treasure. I didn't want to ask Iris to bring anything because she should be resting, so this is fantastic. All I was going to serve was fresh fruit and ice cream. But this makes the meal a feast."

"They're called Nanaimo bars," Kim said.

"Wonderful."

He knew that Nanaimo was a town on Vancouver Island. Was that where she was from? He made a mental note to try and find out more about the elusive Kimberly.

Cooper came bounding out around the side of the house in running shorts and a gray athletic shirt glued to his torso by sweat. Lucky raced toward him, tail wagging, when she saw him, barking joyfully. He looked as happy to see her as she was to see him and James thought that of the two, Cooper was more of a puppy. He was about to make some stupid comment when, to his surprise, a girl jogged in behind his youngest brother. She had long, straight black hair that was tied back, dark eyes, pale skin, and a silver stud in her nose. She was also wearing athletic gear but when she saw the group in the backyard she stopped dead.

Cooper yelled, "Hey, everybody." Then he turned and, finding his friend a few steps behind him, ran back, grabbed her hand and pulled her forward. "This is my friend, Sarah."

The poor girl stopped again and said, "You didn't tell me this was going to be a party."

"It's not, it's dinner with my family. I told you."

She glanced down at herself. "I'm not dressed for company."

With sublime disregard for her obvious embarrassment, Cooper said, "You can shower inside. Come on."

"I haven't got anything clean to wear," and she started to back away.

She might have kept backing all the way off their property if Paisley, his youngest sister, hadn't intervened. With one profoundly disgusted glance in Cooper's direction, she stepped forward. "Hi, I'm Paisley, I think I've seen you around campus?"

The miserable young woman nodded, tugging her shorts down.

"Cooper's clueless, but I've got some clean clothes you can wear. And shampoo and stuff. Come on, I'll show you where everything is."

Things still might have gone badly for Cooper's dating prospects if Daphne hadn't emerged once more from the kitchen and taken in the scene at a glance. "Why hello, you must be Cooper's friend. Looks like you two had a good run."

"I'm so sorry. Cooper didn't explain that it was a party."

"It's not a party. Really. We just have a big family."

"Boys have no clue," Paisley said, "Come on. I'll find something that will fit you."

After the three women went back through the screen door into the kitchen, Rose turned on her baby brother. "Cooper, what were you thinking? That poor girl will never go out with you now."

"What'd I do? I invited her to a family barbecue."

"She didn't know you have the biggest family in Oregon and you drag her in here like she's the winner in a wet T-shirt contest. This is probably the most embarrassing thing that's ever happened to her." Rose, who never went into public without spending an hour on her hair and makeup and had some designer's name associated with every item of clothing and shoes, shuddered. "I feel her pain. I really do."

"Oh, come on," Cooper protested, looking defensive, grabbing himself a beer from the cooler. "That's not the worst thing that ever happened to anyone."

"It could be, it all depends on your perspective. It would be like Matt leaving his scalpel inside a patient. That's the most humiliating thing that could happen to him."

"Hey," Matt said, "Don't put words in my mouth, woman.

Leaving a scalpel inside someone is not my worst nightmare, because I know I'd never do it."

"That's a relief," said Jack who, as well as being his future father-in-law, was also a patient who had once been operated on by him.

"Okay, then, what is the most embarrassing thing that could ever happen to you?" his fiancée asked. Everyone was quiet, listening.

Matt took a slow sip of beer. Considering. "Fainting at the sight of blood, I guess."

Everyone laughed. "But you're a surgeon," Cooper said.

"I know. That's why it would be so humiliating if it ever happened."

"What are we talking about?" Daphne asked, coming back out.

Prescott said, "Most embarrassing thing we could imagine happening. I know the most humiliating thing that could ever happen to me." He turned slowly to where she'd gone to stand with Jack who automatically put an arm around her waist and tucked his spare hand in the back pocket of her jeans, as though they were still teenagers. "It would be having Architectural Digest come here to do a feature on me."

Since James had already had this conversation, he was able to jump in. "Scott's afraid that the readers of his fancy magazines would think he's a cheap ass because he won't design his parents a Prescott Chance Home."

"I'm sorry, sweetheart," Daphne said. "But we love our old place. Which we'll tell those nice folks from Architectural Digest who are coming for that photo shoot next week."

Prescott groaned even as the rest of them laughed.

"How about you, James?" Holly asked, shifting the attention from Prescott and onto him.

He thought about it. "I don't know. Getting shot in the back, I guess, because that would mean I was running away."

"Not the back," Cooper yelled, gleefully, "Getting shot in the butt!"

His extremely mature and classy family found the idea of him getting shot in the butt exquisitely humorous and for once he found himself in charity with Prescott as he and his architect brother shared a glance and simultaneously rolled their eyes.

After chuckling softly, Kimberly said, "I'm sure that will never happen to you."

"I hope not." But then, a week ago, he'd never have imagined he'd ever say to a woman, "We need to talk," which to him was pretty much the verbal equivalent of getting shot in the ass.

CHAPTER 5

"**C**an I get you a beer?" he asked. "Or there's wine or soda."

"A beer would be great, thanks."

He retrieved a beer from the cooler and presented it to her. He was trying to think of something smooth to say when Lauren, who must have snuck back to her car, walked around the side of the house with two tiny furballs clinging to her.

Even as he mentally realized they were kittens, the word, "Kittens!" rang out from every female in sight and suddenly Lauren was surrounded by women plying her with questions and asking to hold the bundles of fluff. Of course, Lucky had also rushed up, but not, he thought in order to gush over the kittens, more to try and chase them or somehow prove Dog the superior animal. She was barking her fool head off.

"This is a cry for help," Lauren admitted when Rose asked, over the sounds of barking, why she had brought kittens to a barbecue.

"Quiet, Lucky. Down," Lauren said, and the dog complied. Lauren's bond with animals was what made her such a great veterinarian. "These babies were brought into our clinic by someone who found them in a box on the side of the road." Her pretty face grew grim. "Who does that? If people had their pets spayed and neutered we wouldn't have such a problem with strays."

"I know, honey," said Jack, who'd managed to edge out the women and somehow got hold of a tiny black and white kitten that he held in the palm of his hand. "What are you going to do with them?"

"These are the last two. I'm trying to find homes for them. I was hoping you might know people who could take a kitten and give it a good home."

"Well, maybe we could…" At that moment Daphne came out, took one look at her husband with the tiny kitten curled up against him and said, "Oh, no."

"But it's homeless. We've never turned away a homeless infant in our lives."

"They were human!"

Iris smoothly intervened. "I could put up a sign in Sunflower. Everyone comes through the coffee shop. We'll have homes for these babies in no time, right, Kim? I'd take one myself if I wasn't expecting twins."

"A sign in Sunflower is a great idea. Especially if it had a picture."

"I'll make you a sign," Daphne offered, clearly hoping to get the kittens housed before Jack talked her into keeping one.

Rose came up to them. "Kim, it's good to see you again. I haven't seen you since the wedding. How are you enjoying Hidden Falls? How's the job going?"

"It's beautiful here. And I love working at Sunflower. Thanks for recommending me."

"Iris has been raving about you. She and Geoff are delighted that you fit in so well."

"That's nice of them to say so."

James said, "I'm not sure if it's fitting in as much as getting dragged in."

Rose nodded. "He's right. If Daphne and Jack take a liking to you, you'll be part of this crazy family whether you like it or not."

He knew that Rose herself hadn't always liked it. She was born cool and elegant. He could still remember when they were kids that she'd somehow make her hand-me-downs look like designer originals. Now that she was a successful doctor, she wore real designer originals.

"That's okay. I like your family."

Jack bellowed, "Burgers are up. Beef, chicken or vegetarian."

Rose ushered Kim toward the food. It was funny how when someone new came among them there was an unspoken rule that one of the family would take the newcomer under their wing. Tonight there were two newbies. Sarah emerged from the house in a loose floral dress that clearly belonged to Paisley. Cooper might have invited his running partner to dinner, but it was obvious that Paisley didn't trust him to take proper care of his guest. The two young women were soon caught up with the kittens and Sarah so quickly settled once she had a fur baby to play with that Cooper was tacitly forgiven.

And then there was Kim. Rose had clearly laid claim to the woman she was responsible for bringing to Hidden Falls. He felt like Cooper, on the outside while the woman he longed to be with was soon settled in a small group with Rose and Iris. He loaded his plate and joined Cooper and the Vasilopoulos brothers.

He and Matt Vasilopoulos had become friends when he'd taken Matt and some buddies shooting as part of a stag outing. That stag party had led to him getting invited to the wedding, which was how he'd met Kimberly.

No doubt Matt saw him glance that way for he said, "Last time I saw Kimberly, you were driving her home from that wedding. Now she's living here in Hidden Falls."

He forked up a chunk of potato salad. "Your two and two

aren't adding up. She didn't know I lived here when she took the job."

"Huh. You two seemed very friendly at the wedding." He bit into a pickle. "Pretty girl."

"All I did was drive her home." Well, there'd been a little more than that, but he wasn't about to share that information with Rose's fiancé. Might as well take out an ad in the Hidden Falls Weekly.

They'd barely finished dinner when Iris yawned hugely. Rose said, "I think this pregnant lady needs to get to bed."

Iris nodded. "I hate to be a party-pooper, but I can't stay awake. But Kim doesn't want to leave this early."

"No. It's fine," Kim said, starting to rise.

"But we haven't even eaten your dessert yet," Daphne protested. "I can drive you home."

"I'll do it," he said.

Kim glanced up at him and he thought she'd refuse, but suddenly she nodded. "That would be great. Thanks."

When, at last, she was settled beside him in his truck and they'd rattled down the rutted lane from his parents' place and onto paved road, he said, "I wasn't sure you'd let me drive you home."

She let out a tiny sigh. "You were right. We do need to talk."

Her tone wasn't enthusiastic, so he kept his tone neutral. "Okay."

She turned her head and stared out the side window, as though the dark fields were fascinating. "I—last time you drove me home, I got carried away. I feel like I might have given you the wrong impression. If I did, I'm sorry." She said it in a rush, as though she'd practiced her speech and wanted to get it out as fast as possible.

He kept his voice deliberately casual. "Hey, it was just a kiss." In fact, it had been one kiss that started out soft and safe and the minute their mouths had met it had turned incendiary. He could still remember the heat they'd generated, the way she'd tasted and the tiny sounds she'd made as the kiss had deepened. One kiss had turned into a string of hungry, open-mouthed soul kisses. He'd had sex that hadn't felt as intimate, or as memorable. They'd both pulled back, shocked at the intensity, and there had been a moment when he'd known, with the certainty that he knew his own name, that if he'd kissed her one more time, they'd be sharing her bed.

However, she'd been skittish and nervous at the wedding. He felt there was something troubling Kimberly and the last thing he wanted was to take advantage of a woman who was under emotional stress and who may have had a drink or two. As much as he'd longed to take things between them to the next level, he wanted to do it right. He'd said he'd call her. And he had. Repeatedly. Until he grew to hate the sound of her recorded message saying she wasn't available. "Not available, I get it," he'd finally yelled at his phone and then forced himself to give up.

She turned and looked at him and he could see that his dismissive tone had surprised her. Which made him smile inside. Her world had been rocked as badly as his had been. So what was the problem? Why had she never answered a single call or text?

"It was a great kiss," she said softly, as though she refused to let him make it less than it was.

"If it was such a great kiss then why have you been avoiding me?"

"I—it's complicated."

"Is there someone else?" He hadn't seen her with a man but that didn't mean there wasn't one.

"No. I just, I don't think it would be good for me to get into a relationship right now."

He turned right toward town feeling better by the second. He heard the longing in her voice, which didn't match her words. "Who said anything about a relationship?" he asked, feeling much more cheerful. "How about we simply enjoy a few more of those steamy kisses?"

He heard a tiny choke of laughter beside him. "Somehow I don't think we'd stick to kissing."

Every fiber of his body perked to attention at the breathless, sexy way she said the words. "Now that's just cruel. You've gone and put a picture in my head of you and me…not kissing."

He felt the air between them crackle with possibilities. "Whereabouts should I drop you?" he asked, as though he hadn't already made it his business to discover where she lived. In a top floor apartment in a brick building from the turn of the last century.

She gave him the cross streets and he nodded.

When he pulled up outside her building, she said, "Thanks for the ride home."

"Kimberly…" All she had to do was lean forward. For a moment their gazes locked, and then, she had the door open and was unbuckling her seatbelt so hastily the truck could have been on fire.

"Thanks for the ride," she said again and was gone.

He waited until she was safely inside, and then pulled away from the curb. He'd confirmed a couple of things tonight. She was single, and that pull between them was as real and powerful as the first time they'd met.

So what the hell was keeping them apart?

KIMBERLY WAS on her hands and knees underneath a table at the Sunflower café. She'd seen the toddler on collision course with her mom's cappuccino (large, low-fat milk, vanilla syrup) before the mom, who was texting somebody on her phone, could register that disaster was imminent. Even as she sprinted from behind the bakery case, the large cup was already on its side and the drink spilling on the floor before she could reach it. Luckily, the hot liquid hadn't splashed the child, her first concern.

The mom, who looked irritable and stressed, put down the phone and turned to the child who had the wrinkled face of a kid about to start wailing. Before Mom could snap at her, which Kim could see was about to happen, she was there righting the cup and saying, "I'll get you another. I'm so glad nobody was hit with the hot milk."

The mom gave her a momentarily puzzled look and then, obviously realizing that a burn on her baby's tender flesh would've been a lot more serious than a spill, said, "Right. Thanks."

"I'll clean this up before anybody slips." And then she dropped to her hands and knees and began mopping up the mess. She heard the jingle of the cheerful sunflower chimes that indicated a customer had entered. It was the strangest thing, but her entire body felt like it sizzled for a moment, almost as though she'd gone radioactive. From her perch underneath the table she peeked out and saw jeans and boots. Even though he wasn't wearing his uniform, she knew it was James Chance. She couldn't explain how she recognized his calves or his boots, but she did. She took an extra moment underneath the table and then backed out.

As she stood, she found that James was looking at her. She had the uncomfortable feeling that he had recognized her based on her butt. As their gazes connected, she nodded and then hastened with her dripping cloth back behind the counter. She threw the sodden cloth in the sink, knowing she would need to get the mop out to finish the cleaning. But first, she started remaking the cappuccino. She also started a small hot chocolate for the little girl.

James didn't say a word. She knew he'd taken in the whole scene when he walked behind her and said softly, "I'll get the mop."

She felt as though he'd given her a bouquet of red roses. "Thanks," she replied, as softly. By the time she returned to the table with the newly made drinks, calm had been restored. James was chatting with the young mother in a manner that Kim frankly thought could be called flirting. The mother was eating it up like the froth of her cappuccino, flicking her hair and smiling at him as though he was the most fascinating man in Hidden Falls. Which, of course, he was. Even the child seemed smitten by his charm and watched with big eyes. He'd finished mopping and stood with his hands around the handle of the mop almost as though it was a trusted friend or a deputy.

She delivered the drinks and got a much calmer thank you from the mom and a shy smile from the little girl and then headed back behind the display case. James walked behind her once more and returned the mop. She could hear him washing it out in the big sink. He was nothing if not thorough.

Unfortunately, she had a feeling he was just as thorough in his policing. She fussed with the things in the front case, rearranging brownies and lemon dream bars, gathering the half a dozen morning glory muffins that remained into a more appealing arrangement, but really all she was doing was giving her nervous hands something to do. James came to the edge of the doorway between the kitchen and the front area and leaned against it regarding her.

She glanced around but everyone was busy and nobody seemed to be in need of a coffee or coming in the door. It seemed as though they had a moment of relative privacy.

"How's it going?" he asked, immediately throwing her off stride. She felt so guilty around him, always waiting to be accused of something. His perfectly normal question had her dropping the silver tongs so they clattered. She rose and faced him. "I'm fine. Hidden Falls is a very nice town and Iris is wonderful."

He nodded, his eyes serious. "Iris is wonderful. And so is this town. Frankly, I try to keep an eye on them both, keep them safe from any harm." He didn't phrase it is a question but she understood that there was a question hanging in the air.

"I know," she said. It was lame but it was all she could manage. To get his attention onto something else, she pointed to the poster Daphne had made advertising that two homeless kittens needed new families. The photograph was heart-meltingly adorable. "One kitten's already found a home. With Loreen Ludlow."

She and Iris had both encouraged the woman, thinking a pet might take some of her attention off James.

"That's great."

"And Edna May Tittlebury is thinking about taking the other one. It's nice to see a lost baby find a home."

"What time do you get off?"

"Iris is coming back around four and we'll close up. We'll be done by five and then I'm finished for the day."

He nodded. "Okay. How about I swing by after five? Maybe I can take you for a cup of coffee." Then he grinned, the seriousness suddenly replaced by amusement. "I meant, maybe I can take you for a drink or something?" Before she could refuse he said, "There's something we need to discuss."

Her stomach began to sink, drifting slowly down like a rock in deep water. She nodded. "Okay." If he heard her obvious reluctance he didn't comment he merely echoed, "Okay. I'll pick you up here."

She didn't know if Iris had asked her brother to check out the newest hire, or if it was Mrs. Busybody Edna May Tittlebury, but Kim was pretty certain that Sheriff James Chance had typed her name into some policing database and whatever it spat out he didn't like.

She couldn't blame him. She didn't like what policing databases said about her either. She wondered if there was a place in the world where she could get away from the blight of her past?

One thing she was certain of, it didn't look like her safe,

secure future was going to be here in Hidden Falls. Once more, she did what she'd done so many times in the past few years. She got ready to move on. She'd be sad to leave here, sad to leave Iris who needed all the help she could get, and sad to leave this quirky town.

Even more, she'd be sorry to know that there was never ever going to be any hope for her with a man like James. In fact, if there was one man she could never have, it would be the town sheriff.

Suddenly she heard her dad's voice echoing in her head. She'd been sixteen, and during one of their infrequent trips to town for supplies, a young guy at the hardware store had asked where she went to school.

"I'm homeschooled," she'd answered, though in truth most of her learning was self-directed. Her mom didn't have time to teach her anything and her father's skills weren't the kind she wanted to learn.

Luckily, she loved to read and devoured books. The only time she ever saw her mother stand up to her dad was when she insisted that Kim be allowed to go to the mobile library every single time it was in their area.

Books became her friends, her link to the outside world, her hope that there was something better out there.

When he'd seen her talking to the boy, her dad had hustled her out of the hardware store so fast she was nearly dizzy. He waited until they were home and then banged his fist on the kitchen counter and warned his eldest daughter, "We only socialize with our own kind. You hear me? You want to talk to boys, you talk to the boys we know."

She was so angry, all the years of doing as she was told, helping with babies and tending wounds and cooking, of wearing clothes that came ordered from a catalogue, all of it came boiling up. "Losers and drug dealers? No thanks!"

CHAPTER 6

*E*ven though her father was more than a thousand miles away, she braced herself. It didn't matter how far she ran, his shadow followed her everywhere, like a persistent cloud hanging over her, blotting out the light.

And now James, the hottest sheriff to ever pin on a badge, wanted to talk to her. From the look on his face, it wasn't soft kisses and softer words on his mind. She tried to rehearse some kind of explanation, but really, what was there to say? He'd find what he'd find, she'd tell him she wasn't part of the family business. He'd believe her or he wouldn't. But that cloud would linger, as black as a thundercloud.

When Iris returned to the café, Kim forgot her fears about the sheriff's little chat and began to worry about Iris instead. She had been around plenty of pregnant women and assisted with more home births than she cared to recall, and, in her opinion, Iris wasn't looking all that hot. When her boss gave her a tired smile she said, "Why don't you sit down? You look tired."

"Thanks." Iris breathed in and out a few times shallowly. "Honestly, I don't feel so good."

There was one older gentleman in the café. He'd finished his coffee ages ago and his newspaper had dropped into his lap when he'd fallen asleep. She left him napping as he wasn't bothering anybody. The only other occupant of the café was Eric, a budding screenwriter who seemed to spend a lot more of his time in the café that he did anywhere else. He could eke out a single cup of coffee longer than anyone Kim had ever seen, but Iris explained that he was part of her creative writing circle and she let him stay. He was tapping away on his keyboard, earphones plugged into his ears and if his cup wasn't empty, whatever was left had to be stone cold. She said, "Why don't we close early? There's nobody here and I can drive you home."

When Iris nodded in agreement, she knew she was right to worry. She hadn't known Iris very long but it was clear the woman was a very hard worker and not the person to close her business early unless she had a very good reason. She helped her sit down, and patted her knee as though Iris were a hurting child, not her boss, and then she walked over to Eric. She had to wave her hand in front of his face to get his attention but when she explained that Iris wasn't feeling well and they were closing early he looked genuinely concerned. He jumped to his feet and began packing up his equipment. "Is there anything I can do?"

She motioned to the sleeping gentleman. "Can you take him with you? I need to help Iris."

"Done." He glanced over at Iris and said, "You tell her, if there's anything I can do, anything at all, to call me."

She nodded, feeling ashamed of how uncharitable she'd been to a guy who was obviously very fond of her boss.

While Eric woke up the old man and got him to his feet, she went back to Iris who was holding her hands over her lower belly. She pulled up a chair close to her employer and said, "Should we call your doctor?" She wasn't sure. Where she came from, calling the doctor was the last resort. Usually, the women handled these things themselves. Iris said, "I don't want any fuss. I just overdid it today. I'll go lie down."

The bell tinkled merrily as Eric opened the door and ushered the older man out of the café, and then turned the Open sign over so it read Closed.

"All right. Let's get you standing and I'll take you home."

Iris pushed up from the table and wobbled. As Kimberly reached out to help her, Iris moaned and her knees buckled as she fainted. *Oh, no.* Kim grabbed her and eased her to the floor. In horror, she noticed there was blood on the seat Where Iris had been sitting.

She stripped off her apron and made a makeshift pillow which she slipped under Iris's head. Then she ran to the coat rack where a yellow sweater had been hanging ever since she started working here. She tucked the woolen garment around Iris's torso and as she did Iris stirred and said, "What happened?"

"You fainted. How many weeks along are you?" Kim asked in a conversational tone. At least she hoped it was conversational and not filled with the mounting fear that consumed her.

"Almost thirty."

Which was not long enough for the twins to have a great chance if they were born now.

As though she had picked up on Kim's thoughts, Iris cried, "I'm not going into labor! I can't be going into labor! It's too early."

Even though her instinct was to tell Iris that everything would be fine, Kim didn't believe in lying. She said, "You sit tight, I'm going to call for help."

She didn't wait for an answer, but the way Iris was lying, with her arms wrapped around her belly and her eyes closed, Kim felt that she had gone inward. She raced to the kitchen wall phone and banged her fingers on the keypad.

"911, what is your emergency?"

"I'm at the Sunflower Coffee and Tea Company in Hidden Falls. I have a pregnant lady here who is bleeding heavily and losing consciousness."

There were way more questions than she had the patience for and she wanted to scream at the woman to just send the damned ambulance right now, but she held it together and answered as best she could. The annoyingly calm voice on the other end said, "I am dispatching an ambulance to your location. Please stand by."

"How long will it take?" She could hear the panic in her tone.

"We'll get there as soon as we can, ma'am."

She ran back out to the front. On the way she grabbed a bundle of tea towels and a bottle of water.

She uncapped the bottle and passed the water to Iris. "Try and drink a little water." She felt that staying dehydrated had to be important and at least it would give them something to do. While Iris drank she said, "The ambulance is on its way."

Iris nodded, looking pale and frightened. Kim had no idea how long it would take an ambulance to arrive. She began to wonder if she'd be better off bundling Iris in her car. She contemplated doing that when she saw a familiar and very welcome face at the door almost before his fist began banging. She jumped up and ran to the door, opening it to let James in.

He glanced at her and then at his sister lying on the floor. In a low voice he asked, "What happened? I heard the dispatcher over my scanner."

To James she didn't disguise the panic she felt. Keeping her voice equally low she said, "She's bleeding, and she passed out."

"Shit. Tell me what I can do to help?"

He seemed to accept that she was in charge of the situation and not he and so she asked, "How long will it take till the ambulance gets here?"

"Less than five minutes."

"Then go talk to her. I'll wait for the ambulance." She nibbled her lip. "Should we call her husband?"

He nodded. "Did it on the way over."

She watched as he strode over and dropped to his knees

beside his sister. "Hey, what's up?" He clasped her smaller hand with both of his.

Iris gave him a tired smile. "I'm not feeling so good."

"Ambulance is on its way, we'll get you feeling better real soon."

As though he'd made the emergency vehicle appear, the sounds of the siren grew louder and within moments an ambulance pulled up outside. She opened the door and ushered in two paramedics holding a stretcher.

While they were examining Iris, James came over and stood with Kim. "Is she going to be okay?" She thought it was interesting that he deferred to her as an expert and also that clearly he was more worried about his sister than his prospective nieces or nephews. She said, "I don't know. She's bleeding, which is not good. It's pretty early for those twins to survive outside of the womb. But miracles happen every day."

He grabbed her hand and squeezed it. "Thank God you were here and reacted so fast. Thank you."

Even though she understood he had only grasped her hand in a moment of stress, she still liked the safe, warm feel of his hand wrapped around hers. She allowed herself a moment to enjoy that warmth and then eased her hand away. "All I did was call 911."

He shook his head. "You kept her warm, you tried to keep her hydrated and you kept her company. I see a lot of emergencies, and those things matter."

They stood together as the paramedics stabilized their patient.

As they lifted the stretcher and James pulled the door open for them, Geoff came running toward them, looking frantic. "That's my wife! What's going on?"

Even as James stepped forward, one of the paramedics spoke. "She's stable, sir. But there's some hemorrhaging. We're taking her to the hospital."

Geoff reached out to touch Iris's shoulder. "I'm here, Babe."

"Oh, Geoff, it's too early. I'm so scared."

"I'm here," he said. "We'll get through this."

As they loaded Iris into the back of the ambulance, the same paramedic looked back at James and Kim. "We can only take the husband."

James nodded. "We'll follow in my truck." He didn't even suggest that Kim stay behind or get dropped off at her place. He assumed she'd want to be with Iris, shared his worry with her as though she were part of the family. Or at least a friend. And he was right.

She grabbed her bag and jacket and Iris' things, locked the door and jogged along with him to his truck.

As they drove to the hospital, he said, "Iris is one of the most amazing people I know."

"Yes."

"She really cares about people, and she listens when anyone has a problem."

She knew he was processing his worry in his own way so she let him tell her how great Iris was, agreeing with everything. "She does."

"She's going to be okay isn't she?"

Once more, she refused to make promises she couldn't keep. She said, "She's going to the best place."

"Thank God you were there," he said again. He turned and his eyes burned into her. "I don't know what would have happened it you hadn't been there when she needed you."

CHAPTER 7

*J*ames paced up and down in the small waiting room of Hidden Falls Hospital. He glanced up and caught Kim's sympathetic gaze on him and smiled wryly. "I know, wearing a trench into the floor won't help Iris but at least it gives me something to do."

She nodded. Gestured to the magazine in her lap. "I'm reading a crochet pattern for a Santa cushion. And I don't even crochet."

He took a couple of steps and then sat on the brown vinyl chair beside her. Her hair was still tied back and it made her look so young. He said, "You barely even know Iris. I don't know why I brought you with me. I just assumed you were coming."

For a moment a look of hurt crossed her face. "I did want to come. I care about Iris. I want to be here."

She was so confusing. If only he could understand what went on behind that flyaway blonde hair and those all too innocent blue eyes. There was a conversation he had intended to have with her today. He had so much emotion rolling around inside of him. Maybe this was as good a moment as any to have that conversation. He took a breath.

In his line of work he had a lot of difficult conversations. He had been the one to tell families of accident victims that their loved ones weren't coming home, explain to wives that their husbands were going to jail, he'd arrested hundreds of perps in his time, so why was this conversation so difficult?

Finally, he plunged in. "I checked up on you."

She did not look all that surprised, simply gazed at him steadily. Then she nodded, "I thought you might."

"Kim, you're an associate of a known drug dealer. Honestly, I thought you were nervous around me because you were scared of uniforms. It's not that, is it? It's because I'm a cop."

She closed her eyes briefly and looked as though she were in pain. She said, "If I had known you lived here in Hidden Falls I never would have come."

That was obvious enough. He'd been drawn to Kimberly since the first moment he saw her. It wasn't only her look of vulnerability and frailty, but something more. She was like a fairytale character; all dressed in rags but underneath she was pure princess.

However, he had an awful feeling that in this case she was the reverse fairytale. She looked like a lost princess but dig a little deeper and he discovered the dark underbelly of corruption. Not every fairytale, he reminded himself, had a happy ending.

He felt suddenly, furiously angry with her. "I don't know what to do," he exploded. "Obviously, my sister should not be hiring people associated with drug lords, but I see you in there with the customers, and you're terrific. Iris says you can bake as well as she can."

A tired smile lit her pale face and she shook her head modestly.

"Why don't you tell me what's going on?"

She looked so sad, so sad he wanted to pull her into his arms and tell her that everything was going to be okay, except that it wasn't.

"I can't. I know it's hard for you to understand but I have

loyalties. Please believe me, I have never knowingly broken the law. Not ever." She gazed at him as though she expected him to believe her and, oddly, he did.

He was also a cop. "So, if you're so innocent, why can't you tell me how your name lit up like a freakin' Christmas tree in my database?"

She shook her head. "Your database doesn't lie." She looked as though someone had let a little air out of her. She slumped in her seat and placed the magazine carefully on the table beside her. Then she said, "I'm leaving, okay? You don't need to worry about me."

"But–"

She stood up. "In fact, I'm going to go home right now and pack. Please tell Iris I'll call her tomorrow and try to explain."

And that irritated him even more. "What about Iris? You can't abandon her." She had already started walking away from him. He leapt to his feet and followed her. He walked so fast that, with his longer stride, he got all the way around her and then turned so he was facing her. If she wanted to keep walking she was going to bump smack into him.

She glared at him.

She took a step, and then another step, and he still didn't move. They were so close that he could see the fine texture of her skin and hear the soft breath she let out. She looked like a woman whose access to the exit door has been cut off which, in fact, it had. She threw up her arms. "What do you want me to do?"

He wanted her not to be a drug dealer, he wanted her to be the sweet, nervous woman he'd first met. He wanted to be holding her in his arms so badly that before he even realized what he was doing he had reached out and pulled her towards him. Before she could protest he slammed his mouth down on hers.

The moment their mouths met, what little sanity he had left in stock fled. Her lips trembled slightly under his. For a moment he felt her go rigid and waited for her to pull away and then, with a tiny sob in her throat, she threw her arms around him and hugged him back, kissing him with all the passion he had felt between them from the first moment.

She pulled away first, her eyes wide and shining with a mixture of passion and horror. "I can't do this."

She stepped around him and this time he let her go. As she headed towards the elevator he yelled, "You can't leave. Iris needs you."

She had reached the elevator and jammed the button with her finger. She turned, a wry smile twisting her lips. "How can I stay?"

And then he said the truest words he knew. "Because I want you to."

THE ELEVATOR DOOR OPENED AND, before Kim could step into it, bodies and noise burst out, filling the narrow corridor. Rose, his sister and favorite GP, pushed out of the elevator first. She glanced from Kimberly to him and said, "Everything we know. Tell me now."

She was in Dr. Crisis Mode, which he respected, but he couldn't get his thoughts straight about exactly what was going on.

Behind her came her fiancé Dr. Matt Vasilopoulos and with them were Jack and Daphne, holding hands as though they could hold each other up through any crisis. He realized they'd been doing that ever since he could remember, holding hands to support each other through all the tough times as well as the good ones.

Before he could marshal his thoughts, Kimberly said, "We don't know a lot yet. Dr. Bailey is with her and I know they called in an OB/GYN. We called the ambulance because she was bleeding and she passed out."

Rose dealt with pregnancies both easy and difficult all the time. She nodded. Taking it in. "What's the status on the babies?"

Kim shook her head. "We don't know. Geoff's the only one they allowed in there but no one's come out to tell us anything."

Rose glanced at her husband-to-be. "I'm going in."

He nodded. "I'll hold the fort here."

She touched his shoulder. "Thanks." Then to their mom and dad she said, "I'll let you know as soon as I find out anything."

At least now that his mom and dad were here, he felt that he could be useful. He said, "I've managed to figure out where the vending machine is. Who wants coffee?"

"Coffee would be good," Jack said.

He headed towards the coffee machine. When he rounded a corner he nearly bashed into Marguerite. "I just heard. Mom called me from the road. How is Iris?"

"We don't know yet. I'm about to get bad coffee for a bunch of people who mostly don't even drink coffee. Will you come and help?"

She nodded. "Sure."

When they returned, Rose was walking into the waiting room and with her was another woman in a lab coat with a stethoscope around her neck. The woman was already talking so he and Marguerite placed the coffees on a handy table and sidled up to listen. "We think they're all going to be fine. We were able to stop the contractions and hemorrhaging. Mom and babies are both doing well. But Iris is going to need to stay with us for a few days until we're absolutely sure everything has settled down. And then she needs to go on absolute bed rest."

Daphne said, "Iris owns the Sunflower Coffee and Tea Company. Can she—"

She didn't even get to finish her sentence before the doctor shook her head. "Absolute bed rest. I don't even want Iris drinking coffee, never mind standing on her feet and making it." She glanced at the group surrounding her and smiled. "You look like people who care about her. You're going to need to be taking her meals in bed, visiting her so she doesn't get too bored. Iris's job is to stay in bed and rest so she can grow those babies. The longer we can keep them inside her, the better chance they have."

"It's not going to be easy keeping Iris away from her business," Jack said.

Geoff spoke for the first time. "Iris wants those babies more than she wants anything." He looked at Kimberly. "She's so grateful that you came along when you did. Can you take over the café until she's back on her feet?"

Kimberly glanced at him before answering, silently asking him not to make trouble for her. Maybe he was a fool to trust her, but it didn't look like any of them had a lot of choice. He'd make it a point to check on her every single day at the café and make sure Iris's trust wasn't misplaced. He gave a slight nod. Then she turned to Geoff. "Tell her not to worry. I can handle it."

The trouble was, now that he had the taste of her on his lips, could he handle it?

CHAPTER 8

*J*ames had discovered when he moved to Hidden Falls that his regular squash games were part of his past. The closest squash court was fifty miles away. So, he took out his frustrations and kept himself in shape by running. He didn't like running, but, besides the obvious attraction of keeping up his fitness, pounding the pavement provided a street-eye view of his community, which was a real bonus to a small town sheriff.

He knew which dogs were all bark and no bite and which ones would rather take a chunk out of a person than issue a warning first. He carried bear spray in a canister swinging from his belt, though he'd only had to use it once. Not on a bear, but on a dog who apparently equated a lone jogger to an attack.

James considered it a win of diplomacy that he was able to convince the owners to keep the dog restrained when they weren't home instead of leaving a bored canine trained to defend its property out in the yard all day. They hadn't realized the dog could jump the fence, or so they claimed when he paid an official visit. Today, he jogged past, bear spray at the ready, but all he heard was the faint aggression from inside the house. Good.

He knew who took pride in their properties and who didn't. He kept a casual eye out for the kind of dangers that could cause trouble in a community. Not only dogs, but poorly stored machinery, anything flammable or sharp that could be misused in the wrong hands.

He jogged on. As they'd prearranged, Geoff McLeod was waiting at the corner near the home he shared with Iris. He was stretching his calves against a street lamp and when he spotted James, he broke into a jog and they headed out together. He liked Geoff. The local high school English teacher was not only his brother-in-law but a genuinely good guy.

"Wasn't sure you'd make it today," he said by way of a greeting.

"After the scare I had last night, I need to get some of this adrenalin out of my system."

"How's Iris?" He'd never forget seeing his sister lying on the floor of her café, pale and obviously in pain. He was glad they'd saved the babies, but in truth, all he'd cared about was his sister.

"She's blaming herself. She should have rested more, shouldn't have done this or that. But the truth is, her cervix just wasn't strong enough to hold the babies in. At least, that's what I think the doc said.

This was way more information about his sister's insides than he wanted. "When's she coming home?"

"They said in a few days. Daphne's great, she's already cooking up a load of casseroles to put in the freezer. She's given me some names of people who can come in to clean and do the housekeeping until I get off school for the summer."

"Good. That's good."

"And Kimberly is amazing. I don't know what we'd do without her. Well, I do, we'd have to close Sunflower and that would stress Iris out almost as much as worrying about the babies."

"Yeah, Kimberly is fantastic." He felt the words grate across his throat. He hadn't been able to stop thinking about that kiss, which should have been the least exciting kiss in history since it had happened in a hospital waiting room while his beloved sister was in the ER. Instead, it was up there with the most exciting moments he'd experienced in his life. He'd lived through entire relationships that didn't contain a single second as exquisite as that moment when he'd felt her give, felt her respond to him with every bit of pent up passion in her. And she had a lot of pent up passion.

He couldn't share with Geoff what he'd discovered, but he wished he could. He'd entered Kimberly's name into a National Crime Information Centre database almost on a whim and had been surprised when he got some pings back from Canada. Kimberly was a known associate of a drug dealer in Nelson, British Columbia. Back in his days as a Seattle cop, he'd dealt with plenty of drug crimes. He'd been part of a JFO, a joint forces operation, with the RCMP in Canada and, knowing he wouldn't rest until he knew more, had called a guy he'd worked with from Vancouver, Corporal Doug Ng. Doug knew the guy in Nelson and came back with the information that Kim was part of the Parker family.

"Nelson's pretty much the marijuana capital of Canada," Doug had informed him. "Frank Parker was a draft dodger, came up here and settled. He's been growing and dealing pot for years. Him and a bunch of his buddies. They live like a commune. Sticking together, working together, protecting each other. Course, he could see the writing on the wall that marijuana would end up legalized, so he branched out."

"Into what?"

"Crystal meth. Maybe cocaine."

Damn it. "Is the daughter dealing?" He knew that however much he was drawn to Kim, he couldn't stand by while a known drug dealer moved into his town. Even if she did have the prettiest blue eyes he'd ever seen and kissed like an angel.

"No proof of that. She's never been busted."

"Thanks."

"Hey, if you know anything, you'll share, right?"

Knowing that Doug had the same instincts as the vicious attack dog where drug dealers were concerned, he gave the truth. "She hasn't done anything illegal. My sister hired her and I did a NCIC check, that's the only reason I was looking at her."

"Okay." Then they'd chatted for a few minutes about how the laws regarding marijuana had changed and how it would change their respective jobs. Seemed like the Parker family was staying firmly in the more lucrative black market even if it meant changing the drugs they peddled.

Of all the people he could have fallen for, did he have to lose his heart to a woman from a drug dealing family?

Could she be planning to bring drugs into Hidden Falls? Was that why she moved so often? Why she looked guilty whenever she saw him? He decided that keeping a close eye on Kimberly Parker would be a very good idea.

"I AM SO glad to see you!" Iris exclaimed as Kim slipped into her room, keeping her footfalls soft in case Iris was sleeping. Iris wasn't sleeping, she was holding a book called Baby's First Month in her hand, but her gaze seemed to be focused on the window, where a maple tree made patterns against the sky.

"Daphne said I should come on up, but I wasn't sure if you'd be sleeping."

"No. I'm not sleeping. I'm not sick. I'm pregnant. And when you're not sick, staying in bed all the time is intensely uninteresting." She sounded petulant which Kim took as a good sign that she was feeling better.

"The babies are okay?"

"Babies are fine. So long as I don't do anything but lie here, the odds are good that we'll get pretty close to full term."

Kim searched her face but Iris looked much better than she had the last week before she'd collapsed. She might feel bored, but it was obvious the rest was good for her as well as the babies. "I'm so glad."

Iris smiled her wide smile. "Me, too. Bored is good. I don't know what would have happened if you hadn't been there, but I'm really glad you were. Thank you."

"All I did was call 911. Anyone would have."

She shook her head. "You caught me when I fell, you talked to me so I wasn't scared. You made a terrifying experience a lot less terrifying, so thank you." Her eyes began to swim and she shook her head to clear them. "Damn hormones. I cry every time I think of how close I came to losing the babies. Sit down, will you? Tell me about Sunflower and take my mind off *me*."

She was happy to oblige. She sat in the chair set up beside the bed that someone had positioned so Iris could talk to her visitor without having to move. The bedroom was a bright, happy space. Painted yellow, the room boasted a huge sleigh bed covered in a quilt with all the colors of a summer garden. Her dressing table was covered with photographs of her family and friends. Kim felt a pang of envy. She couldn't imagine being proud enough of anyone in her family that she'd want photographic evidence. She loved her family, but her feelings were always conflicted by guilt and shame.

She shifted her attention to her carry bag. She drew out a bakery box that would be very familiar to Iris. "I brought you a few things to try." In fact, she'd brought one of everything that she'd baked this morning. Even though she was using Iris's recipes and doing the baking in Iris's kitchen she wanted to make certain that the goods all tasted the same as what Iris was used to.

"Oh, you sweetheart!" Iris exclaimed. "I feel so much better knowing Sunflower is in good hands." She reached for a brownie and bit into it. Not in a critical way as Kim had expected, as though she were a judge in a baking contest, but as someone enjoying a treat. "Oh, yum. You know I'm going to devour every one of these. You can't tell Mom or she'll demand I share."

"I can bring some more," she said, feeling she'd screwed up already.

"I'm joking. I'll share these. But sure, if you come back, bring a few more things. I'm getting so many visitors it will be good to have something to give them."

She hadn't even made one critical comment. Kim couldn't believe it.

"How's it going at Sunflower?" Iris asked.

Kim pulled out the bank receipts she'd been saving. "Here are the deposit slips from the past few days," she said. "I asked Geoff and he told me just to take the money to the bank at the end of each day." She'd been terrified she'd get mugged on the short journey to the bank on the corner but miraculously she'd deposited the day's take without any other incident than being serenaded by a street musician. He wasn't very good, but she put a dollar in his flute case anyway. And got the flute version of a wolf whistle as thanks.

Iris took the receipts and barely glanced at them. "I'm really sorry all this got dumped on you so suddenly. Are you okay? As soon as school's finished Geoff can help out in the bakery and, of course, the high school kids who help out will be available all day. But that's two months from now."

"I'm managing fine, honestly, and everyone in town knows you're on bed rest, so business is booming. They come in to find out how you are and then, of course, feel like they have to buy something. Customers have been so patient about waiting an extra couple of minutes if they need to."

"Good. I talked to Dosana. She'll come when she can get away from the other bakery to lend a hand."

"Great."

"You know what I miss? All the little dramas and short stories that are played out every day in Sunflower. Tell me what's going on."

Kim wished someone from Iris's creative writing circle was here. No doubt they could make the everyday incidents exciting, but she thought hard and did her best to pick a couple of stories that Iris would find entertaining.

"I think the older gentleman, Harold, who comes in every day, might be interested in Edna May Tittlebury," she said at last.

"What?" Iris's eyes lit up and she snuggled against her pillows obviously ready for a good gossip. "Harold Biedleman?"

"I could be wrong, but he's started coming in right around the same time she does. He always pretends that it's a coincidence and then they end up sitting together. Today he bought her a lemon dream bar."

"Oh, my God, I can't believe I'm missing this. That's adorable. Of course, Edna May is the worst gossip in all of Hidden Falls. Oregon probably, so how perfect that she's now the subject of gossip. I love it! What else?"

Soon she was launched into a story about Eric, the young screenwriter. "He says he's started a new screenplay. He was asking my advice."

"Your advice? Do you love horror? Because that's what he writes."

She shook her head, trying to keep the grin off her face. "After you collapsed in the bakery, he realized that true drama isn't the Zombie Apocalypse, it's the stuff that happens every day."

Iris groaned. "I forgot he was there that day. How embarrassing that he saw me pass out."

She shook her head. "He didn't see anything. He was too busy working on his computer and he had headphones on so he never noticed anything until I asked him to scoop up an older gentleman who'd fallen asleep and get them both out of there. He was so sweet when he realized you weren't feeling well. He hustled the old guy out and even put up the Closed sign."

"Well, that was nice of him."

"And now he wants to write a screenplay where you are the heroine."

Iris made a face. "I think he should stick to zombies."

"In his words, 'True horror is when bad things happen to good people.'"

Because they were both laughing, she didn't hear James come in, but suddenly, she felt his presence and glanced up to find his gaze on her. He looked so good in his uniform. Fit and gorgeous and impossible. How she wished he'd never kissed her at the hospital. She kept reliving the moment, wishing she could fall for him all the way.

Iris said, "James, Hi. Did you come to take pity on your poor bedbound sister and bring her community gossip? Or can't you break sheriff/perp confidentiality?"

"I've got nothing as exciting as what happens in the bakery. It's where I go to find out what's happening in town."

He stepped over and kissed his sister on the cheek. Then gently patted the mound of her belly that was getting bigger every day. "How are my nieces and nephews?"

"I'm not sure whether they're going to be twin gymnasts, twin ice skaters or boxers." She took the heel of her hand and pushed against her belly. "Make that kick boxers."

"It's good that they're active, right?" he asked. Kim thought the look of concern on his face was adorable. And sexy.

"Very good. But sometimes they kick so hard they wake Geoff up in the night."

Kim stood up, vacating the visitor chair. "I'll head out now. Here, James, take the chair."

"No. It's fine. I can go help Mom in the kitchen while you finish your visit."

"I'm all out of gossip. It's your turn."

"But you'll come back tomorrow, right?" Iris asked.

"Of course."

As she walked past James on her way out of Iris's bedroom, she caught his gaze on her and his eyes crinkled in a very disturbing way.

She wasn't very surprised when, the next day, the second she walked into Iris's bedroom, Iris said, "So, what's going on with you and my brother?"

"Really? Shouldn't you be asking how many brownies I sold today and whether Harold and Edna May had coffee together?"

"I am much more interested in what's going on with you and Sheriff Chance."

Kim shook her head but felt herself blushing.

"Come on. I saw you two making googly eyes at each other yesterday. Something's happened. I have nothing to do all day but lie here. Give me something, anything."

"Mind your own business."

"I am minding my own business, which is lying here, growing babies. You have to take pity on me. I need gossip, I need intrigue, I need news. And not the kind I can get from CNN!"

And, since she spent so much time with Iris, and considered her a friend as well as her boss, she tried to give her some part of the truth, at least as well as she understood it herself. She sighed, sank into the chair and said, "As I believe I have mentioned, I had a bit of a crush on James when I met him."

"You want my opinion, I'd say the crush is mutual."

"Well, for right now that's all it is. But he comes in every day for coffee." She shifted to get comfortable and grinned. "And, second only to my time here with you, it's the highlight of my day."

CHAPTER 9

*K*im heard a funny noise. For a moment she wasn't certain what it was, and then realized the sound was of her own humming. It was an old John Denver song, Rocky Mountain High, but it wasn't the song that was as remarkable as the fact that she was humming. It was something she used to do when she was happy.

For the first time in a long time she realized that she *was* happy. She had come to love the Sunflower Coffee and Tea Company. As sorry as she was that Iris was stuck in bed, it was nice to be trusted enough to run the bakery, and even better, she knew she was doing a great job.

The customers liked her, the work was satisfying, and with Iris's permission, she had even introduced Nanaimo bars, a layered concoction of a chocolate and coconut base, a middle layer of thick custard and a final topping of chocolate. The bars were from her native Canada and had been pretty popular at the family barbecue. She thought, if she stayed here long enough, she might even try baking maple sugar cookies but she didn't want to push too hard too fast with the cross-border baking.

She visited Iris every day after she closed the bakery. Iris had plenty of friends and family so it wasn't that she lacked visitors, but the Sunflower Coffee and Tea Company was her baby and her passion and she enjoyed hearing the stories of the funny things that happened in the bakery as well as a tally on sales.

Dosana still did all the ordering and Geoff popped in when he could to keep an eye on things but she knew that Iris liked to hear about all the little dramas that played out each day. "It makes me feel like I'm still part of the bakery."

"Oh, believe me, you are." Kim pulled out from her bag yet another greeting card from one of the customers who missed Iris along with a teddy bear. She set it on the table amongst all the other greeting cards and flowers and plush animals. There were always fresh flowers. As one lot drooped another seemed to take its place. And there always seemed to be someone named Chance helping out around Iris's house. At this very moment, the muffled sound of a vacuum cleaner hummed from downstairs, and when she'd said her hellos as she walked in, she'd discovered Marguerite on the phone to Rose, giving the Portland GP the daily update. She'd never seen a family that worked so well together and she experienced a tinge of envy.

Beneath the covers of Iris's bed, she could see that the mound of her pregnancy was growing nicely. Following her gaze, Iris patted her own belly and said, "Today's a big day. I officially passed the thirty-five week mark. If I can hold the suckers in one more week it will be considered full-term."

"That's great. How are you feeling?"

Iris's hand rubbed absently up and down her belly. "I feel fat, overwhelmed, and scared." She shifted uncomfortably. "And I swear these two are going to be fighting all the time. I think that's all they do in the womb. Fight all day." She took Kim's hand and placed it on her belly. "Can you feel them?"

She laughed, softly. "Feel them? It's like a whole litter of puppies rolling around in there. Are you sure it's only two?" she teased.

Iris groaned. "I can only handle two." And then she nibbled her lip. "In fact, I'm not even sure I can handle two. Or even one! I don't know how to be a mother at all."

"I think it's one of those jobs where the babies provide on-site training." She patted Iris's belly and withdrew her hand. "You're going to be fine." She hesitated and then said, "Back home, I've seen plenty of women give birth who are a lot less ready than you are. Somehow, they figure it out. You will too."

"You never talk about your background."

She was sorry now that she'd said anything at all. "It's really not very interesting."

"Compared to, say, lying here in bed all day every day? You think your story's not interesting? Trust me. I'm fascinated. I've watched all seven seasons of *The Good Wife* on Netflix, gobbled up *Scandal*, even though I'd already seen it when it came out. I think I got through *The Gilmore Girls* in a week. Trust me, I need a new story."

And she thought, why not? She and Iris were friends, and Iris had a way about her that made a person want to unload their problems, share their secrets. "I would really appreciate it if what I tell you went no further."

Iris looked first puzzled and then concerned. "Okay."

She gazed out of the window and saw pretty trees that were part of an orderly neighborhood surrounded by nicely kept houses.

"I never tell people about my past. I am seriously trusting you." And maybe it was time.

"You can, you know."

She drew in a breath and said, "My dad was a draft dodger. He settled in a little town in British Columbia, near Nelson. He had a buddy up there who'd told him about the place." She began to tell the story that shamed her to her core. "They started a grow op. Back before they were even called grow ops. A few more of their friends moved up and they began buying up acres of land and growing cannabis. It's what our family lived on. Black market marijuana." After marijuana started to be legalized, she'd hoped her dad would retire. But he was too used to the easy money. Her mother was close-lipped about his activities, but Kim was worried that branched out. She couldn't condone his behavior and she couldn't turn him in, so she felt stuck between loyalty and conscience. Every time she read about an overdose she wondered where the victim got their drugs from.

"Wow."

"My mom is a lot younger than my dad. She came up to visit and they hooked up." Her mind drifted back to the life she had left. "They didn't have as many kids as your folks, only six. I'm the oldest, so I always helped out. Where we grew up, you kept to yourself. I was taught from an early age the cops were the enemy. They didn't even let doctors come out to our property. I can't think of one woman in our circle who went to a hospital to have her baby. They had them at home."

Iris had both hands on her belly now. "It sounds like it was awful."

She shrugged. "I didn't know any better. And one thing's for sure, you get pretty good at doing for yourself. I've helped birth a lot of babies. My first aid skills are pretty good. I can stitch up a cut if it's not too bad. And, of course, I've been baking since before I could read."

"It's like you time-travelled from the time of the early settlers or something."

"Sometimes I feel like that. We lived like the Amish, without their decency."

Iris suddenly reached out and put a hand on her knee. "It wasn't your fault. You were a little kid."

"I know but, now that I'm older, I see the evil that drugs do. Drug money clothed me and fed me. Anyway you look at it, I was part of that."

"I made the mistake of tracking down my birth parents." At

Kim's surprised glance she said, "Jack and Daphne made a rule that if we wanted to know if we were their natural children or adopted that we had to wait until we were sixteen. Then it was up to us. So, when I was sixteen, I asked. Mom, Daphne, cried when she told me and I think I cried too."

"That must have been so hard for you both."

Iris nodded. "I found my birth parents and let me say that the best thing they did was give me up." She shook her head as though she could shake off a bad memory. "But what if my mom hadn't? I'd have been raised with a single mom who only got pregnant to try and get her married lover to leave his wife and move in with her. Didn't work out the way she planned it, but it could have. I was so lucky to end up where I did. I think you have to accept that you didn't have a choice. You got through a tough childhood the best way you could and now you live your own life."

"But my family, all our friends' families, they're criminals."

Iris gazed at her steadily. "Is that why you're so weird around James?"

When Iris mentioned her brother's name, Kim felt the longing for James that she couldn't ignore. He was the last man she could have, and the only one she wanted. "Like I said, my whole life I've been taught to stay far away from cops."

"James is a good man. He'd understand that whatever your parents do it's not your fault." A troubled expression crossed Iris's face. "If only his partner–"

"If only his partner what?"

Iris shook her head. "Not my story to tell. I shouldn't have said anything. I'm not myself today."

She wanted to press, to try and find out more about what had happened to James's partner. She had a bad feeling that it wasn't a story with a happy ending, but Iris shifted again, clearly uncomfortable. "The babies feel so heavy."

"How many weeks along did you say you are?" She'd seen that

look on a woman's face before. It was a kind of inward -looking, pensive expression that suggested to Kim that those squirming babies were getting ready to make an early entrance into the world.

"Thirty-five weeks."

"When is your next appointment with the OB/GYN?"

Iris shifted again, and for a moment Kim wasn't certain that she'd heard her. Then she said, "Monday, I think. Maybe Tuesday." She shifted again. "My back hurts. I think it's from lying here so much. My muscles are probably atrophying."

Kim didn't stay much longer, and when she went downstairs, she found Daphne in the kitchen arranging dark purple spears of Iris in a tall vase. She glanced up when she saw Kim and her blue-green eyes lit up as she smiled her big, welcoming smile. "I know she doesn't need more flowers, but I saw these at the market today and, well, they are not only very pretty but her namesake flower."

"I'm sure they will cheer her up."

Daphne dropped her tone to an almost conspiratorial whisper and said, "Look what else I have." From a plain brown paper bag she withdrew two tiny layette sets exquisitely knitted. One was yellow and the other white. "I could not resist. Do you think I can give them to her now? I know we agreed not to have a baby shower until after the babies are born, but I don't think it's bad luck to give these to her now, do you?"

Kim could not remember a time when she had felt so included. It was like this big happy Chance family had simply accepted her into their fold, when she was only Iris's employee. And now, here was Daphne asking her advice, as though she were Iris's intimate friend instead of a woman who'd only been working here a couple of months.

She picked up a pair of the yellow knitted booties. "They're so tiny. You can never quite believe that a little human being will fit into these."

Daphne nodded. "And then they'll grow out of them so fast your head will spin, but I am grabbing my grandmother's right to buy foolish and impractical baby gifts."

She thought about Iris upstairs with her aching back and restlessness and said, "I think you should give them to her today. I'm not as experienced as you are, I've never had a baby of my own, but I don't think the babies are going to wait much longer."

Daphne had a way of looking at her as though she could see behind Kim's façade to the frightened little girl she still was deep inside. She said, "I think you are someone who sees a great deal more than she lets on."

She didn't say anything at all just continued to trace the pattern of the tiny yellow booty in the palm of her hand.

"You've helped Iris more than just in the bakery and we all know it. You may not want to hear this, but you're fast becoming one of us. Like family."

She shook her head. "I could never be part of your family." She heard the sadness behind her words and probably Daphne could too.

"A family is more than a collection of matching DNA. Our kids came to us in a variety of ways, but every one of them belongs. Who's to say you don't belong here, too?"

Kim glanced up at her in surprise. She was more and more convinced that this woman actually could read minds. If she hadn't just left Iris, after telling her about her own history, she'd have believed that Iris had blabbed all her secrets to her mom. But, obviously that wasn't the case. Somehow, Daphne had seen through her to the lost little girl who was still trying to find her place in the world.

She placed the booties carefully back on the white tissue they'd been wrapped in and said, "Your kids were very lucky. Every one of them."

Daphne rewrapped the tiny bundles of clothing and replaced them inside the bag. "We were all lucky."

She wanted to ask more questions, to imagine for a moment what it would've been like growing up with Jack and Daphne as parents, but before she could form her first question, Geoff walked in carrying reusable cloth bags heaping with groceries.

"Hello, ladies!" He announced cheerfully. Emerging from one of the bags was a string-tied bundle of purple irises.

He glanced at the irises Daphne had just finished placing in the vase and his grin widened. If ever a man had looked pleased with himself and happy about his impending fatherhood, Geoff had to be that guy. "Great minds," he said.

Daphne was folding over the rim of the bag containing the knitted layettes, Geoff was heading for the kitchen counter beside the fridge and Kim was thinking she should leave, when all of them froze at the sound of a strangled scream.

Geoff dropped both bags of groceries from nerveless hands and began to sprint for the stairs.

"Oh my God!" Daphne whispered before following her son-in-law. Kim hesitated for a second, then grabbed her cell phone and also headed for Iris. As she left the kitchen, she stepped over the groceries. A gallon jug of milk now lay on top of the cheerful purple irises.

When she reached Iris's room, her pounding heart eased a little as she immediately took in the situation. Iris was leaning on Geoff, her face flushed and her breath coming in pants. "I think my water broke."

Daphne said in a wavering voice, "Oh, honey. It's time."

Geoff held his wife, in her damp nightgown, as though she were the most precious thing in the world. "Let's get you to the hospital."

Kim came into the room quietly and said, "Why don't I help Iris get into some dry clothes, and you call ahead to the OB/GYN so she can meet you at the hospital?"

They all looked at her. Iris nodded. "I do not want to show up at the hospital in a dripping nightgown. There are some dry sweats in the middle drawer."

Geoff was already reaching for his cell phone. "I'll call ahead."

"What should I do?" Daphne asked, looking at Kim.

"I think you should call your husband and tell him he's about to be a grandfather. And then maybe let the rest of the family know."

"Right." Daphne stepped towards Iris and patted her shoulder. "You'll do great. And as soon as the babies are born, we'll be waiting to welcome them into our family."

Iris fell into her mother's arms. "I've wanted this day for so long, I can't believe it's finally here."

They were on their way within ten minutes, Iris looking nervous but excited as Geoff helped her to the car. Daphne waved them goodbye and then got on the phone. Kim picked up the dropped groceries and put them away. The flowers weren't too bad. She threw away the two broken stems and added the rest to the vase Daphne had already partially filled.

"Please let Iris and her babies be all right," she whispered aloud.

CHAPTER 10

*K*im returned to her tiny apartment but she couldn't settle. She tried to read, but the words swam in front of her eyes and she reread the same paragraph so many times that eventually she gave up. She flipped on the television and soon flipped it off again. Finally, she did what she always did when she was troubled or couldn't sleep—she baked.

Around three a.m. she was startled by a knock on her door. This was supposed to be a secure building but most of the time the front door was unlocked. Hidden Falls was a small town and it seemed very safe but still she put her eye to the peephole. Her eyes widened but that didn't change who was on the other side of her door. James.

She opened it saying eagerly, "Any news?"

She could tell right away that he had good news for he couldn't seem to keep the smile off his face. "Mom and babies are both safe. It's a boy," he paused for dramatic effect "and it's a girl! I know it's the middle of the night, but I saw your light on. I'm so wired, I had to tell someone."

Her eyes filled with foolish tears. "Oh my gosh, I'm so glad everybody's okay. How was the birth?"

He shook his head. "If you want the gory details, you'll have to ask her yourself. I've been to triple murder scenes that didn't freak me out as much as what Iris has been through." He stood there, looking solid and yummy in jeans and a plaid shirt. His face was stubbled and there were circles under his eyes but he was obviously filled with energy. "I hope you don't mind me stopping by so late."

"No. I've been wondering who I could call for an update. Thank you."

They stood staring at each other stupidly for a minute and then he said, "It smells great in here. Have you been baking?"

She lifted her flour-streaked hands helplessly. "It's what I do when I'm nervous. You want to come in? I have fresh muffins. I can put on some coffee." She checked the wall clock. "I have to head for the bakery in about an hour anyway. I could use some coffee."

"Yeah. That would be good." He walked in and shut the door behind him. She measured out coffee, water, keeping her hands busy while she was acutely aware of him.

He said, "You must've been very nervous." As she glanced behind her shoulder she understood what he meant. She had baked a lot. Two kinds of muffins, a stack of peanut butter cookies, and another of chocolate chip, which she'd done on autopilot because their homey scents always calmed her. Two loaves of whole grain bread hulked on a cooling rack and a pie oozed purple through its lattice crust.

"Are those Iris's morning glory muffins?" he asked.

"No. They're my own recipe. Give them a try and tell me what you think."

The coffee began to bubble and gurgle behind her, putting one more delicious smell into the room. James did not wait for his coffee, he reached for one of the muffins and ripped it cleanly in half, releasing a puff of steam.

"Butter's in the pottery dish beside you," she said sliding open the cutlery drawer and passing him a knife.

He shook his head and then bit into the muffin. He ate the way he seemed to do everything, cleanly, efficiently, with no wasted movements. When he'd swallowed the first bite he said, "this is delicious. I love Iris's morning glory muffins but I have to tell you, this is every bit as good."

She felt as pleased as if she'd won the blue ribbon in a baking contest. "Glad you like them."

He glanced at her curiously. "You sound as though my opinion matters."

She placed a small white plate in front of him and one in front of herself, added blue cloth napkins. "Being a baker must be the ultimate occupation for a pleaser," she admitted.

His gaze was quietly intense. "Are you a pleaser?"

There was no particular intonation to his words, but still she felt them dance intimately across her skin. She imagined what it would feel like to please him and to let him pleasure her.

She crossed to the coffee machine so she wouldn't have to face him when she answered. She took her time pouring coffee into white mugs as she said, "I want people to enjoy the foods I bake. I hate conflict and get nervous when anyone's angry with me, so I guess that defines me as a pleaser."

"Do people get angry with you very often?"

She didn't ask him if he wanted milk in his coffee, but dug a carton out of the fridge, poured milk into a pitcher and put it, with the matching sugar bowl, on the counter beside him. "Not so much. Not anymore."

"Did someone used to be angry with you?" He said the words gently, but she wasn't going down this road. Not with him. Not now.

"Is this a friendly visit or an interrogation?"

He poured milk into his coffee and, to her surprise, added two heaping spoons of sugar. As he stirred his coffee he said, "Maybe you're not as bad at conflict as you think."

She added a much smaller amount of both sugar and milk to her coffee and reached for one of the muffins. "Tell me about the babies."

He looked at her for a long second, then, obviously accepting that she was going to avoid his question, he pulled out his phone. "Don't worry, there's no birthing video on here. Only some pictures of Mom and the babies. My niece and nephew. I can't get over it."

He fiddled with the phone and then moved to sit beside her, so close she could smell the clean, masculine smell of him. Feel the warmth coming off his muscular arm as he leaned in to share the small screen with her. For a second her senses were too addled to focus, and then she did and let out a small sound of happiness. "Oh, look at them. They're so small and so perfect."

Two little squished faces stared out from under impossibly tiny cotton caps, one blue and one pink. "Are they all right? Not too small? Are their lungs developed enough to be outside?"

"You sound like Rose!" He flipped to the next photo, Geoff holding their daughter and a tired but very happy looking Iris holding their son. "Everything's great. They're a little on the small side, which I'm told is typical for twins. One's five pounds and one's a little less. The lungs are fine. All that bed rest paid off."

"I'm so glad. Have they got names yet?" Geoff and Iris had pored through baby naming books and come up with and rejected hundreds of boy and girl names.

"I think they've settled on Mia Daphne for the girl and Liam John, for the boy, for both the grandfathers."

"Oh, those are beautiful names."

She turned and found him so close she could see a small scar across one eyebrow that she'd never noticed before. It fascinated her. Where had he got it? How many stitches? Was it a work injury?

So close she could lean over and kiss him without any effort at all. The atmosphere changed and she knew he'd read her mind or come to the same thought independently. Her lips began to tingle and she felt her pulse kick up. He leaned in a fraction and then all the reasons why this was a terrible idea rushed at her. She pulled back. "How did you get that scar?" she asked, as though she'd been thinking of that and not how his mouth would feel against hers. How much she wanted to wrap herself in his warmth and strength and simple goodness. "The one on your eyebrow."

He blinked. Once. And then raised a hand to the old wound as though he'd forgotten it was there. "It was a twin thing. Something Iris and Geoff are going to have to get used to. Josh and I were both on the swim team in high school. He was a way better swimmer than I was, but we were competitive about everything. Except girls, obviously, since he's gay. Anyway, we had a race."

He grinned in memory. "I was not being a good sport, trying to elbow him and kick him underwater and generally acting like an ass. He took it for a while and then finally came right into my lane and we got into it. Both nearly drowned before I hit my head on the pool edge, which broke my goggles, which cut my eyebrow. There was blood all over the place, very dramatic. The fight drew a small crowd of classmates. A couple of them dragged me out of the water, with Josh pushing from below and this girl, Kelly McCutcheon, who'd recently finished her lifeguard training, insisted on giving me the kiss of life." He scratched his stubbled jaw. "I was breathing fine, but she kissed me anyway. For quite a long time. I think we dated for three months, which is an eternity in high school."

She smiled at the story and definitely understood where Kelly McCutcheon was coming from. "Did you need stitches?"

"Oh, yeah. I looked pretty gruesome for a couple of weeks.

Josh walked around like he was Rocky himself and Kelly spent a lot of time kissing me better."

She shook her head at him. "You were lucky you didn't lose an eye."

"It's amazing what kids get away with. How about you? You must have some good high school stories from Canada. Were you on the hockey team?"

She shook her head.

"Ski team?"

"No."

"Dog sled team?"

"Canada is not an Arctic wasteland, you know."

"I know. So, you must have been on some school team."

"I was homeschooled." She glanced at the clock. "And I have to get ready for work."

He grabbed a peanut butter cookie as he stood up. "You know, Iris never starts this early."

"I know, but I'm making something special this morning. To celebrate. The way gossip flies in this town, we'll be packed with customers wanting to share her good news. Your sister has gone through labor and birthed two babies. I figure she should profit off the gossip." She had an idea. "Can you print off a cute baby picture and bring it to Sunflower? I'll pin it up on the wall."

"Sure. Happy to be of service."

She packed him a goodie bag of cookies and muffins telling him to take them to work with him. "Remember, Connie loves chocolate. Make sure she gets some chocolate chip cookies."

As he was leaving, he said, "You know, Iris made a good choice when she hired you."

After the suspicious way he'd treated her she was flattered. "So, you don't think I'm here to cause trouble?"

His eyes grew intense on hers. "Oh, you are definitely trouble," and then, before she even saw it coming, his mouth slammed down on hers in a take-no-prisoners kiss that was as intense as it was brief.

He raised his head and when their gazes connected she could not pull away. She read his intent even as he came closer and still she did nothing to stop the inevitable. She made a tiny sound of acceptance in her throat. And when he pulled her back into his arms, she felt such a tsunami of desire that her feelings rocked her to her toes. Why? Why of all men did it have to be a cop she had this intense reaction to? She'd tried to fight her wild attraction, but it was hopeless. As he pulled her tight against him and she felt all the hard planes and angles of his body and the way her own softness yielded, she let herself go.

She was always so careful, always on the run, never letting anyone get too close. But since she had arrived in Hidden Falls, it seemed as though all her careful defenses were being knocked down, one by one.

She'd accepted friendship, told secrets that no one but her own family knew, opened herself up in so many ways, but this? Falling for the town sheriff? This had to be the stupidest thing she'd ever done. But, even as she understood how stupid it was, she still pressed herself against James.

While his mouth was busy on hers, exciting, teasing, drawing out helpless sounds from deep in her throat, his hands were busy touching, teasing, exciting. Her hands were just as busy. She loved the hard angles and tight muscles. She felt oddly safe in his arms. James was a born protector. For a woman who had been on her own and frightened for so long, a strong, protective man seemed deceptively good. Of course, in her head, she understood that he was the most dangerous man she could know, but her body didn't respond that way.

She slid her hands under his shirt needing to feel his warm, naked skin. Knowing, that this time, there was no going back.

She began to yank his T-shirt upwards and then his hands joined hers and helped pull the shirt over his head. She buried her lips in the closest part of his chest that she could reach, which was the dip in his collarbone above where the strong musculature of his chest was covered by exactly the right amount of dark brown chest hair.

While she was busy exploring the contours of his chest with mouth and hands he was busily helping her out of her shirt. And then he had her bra off with a deftness that surprised her. She barely felt the back give and then her bra was gone, exposing her. Had she ever been this aroused? She didn't think so.

Desire licked at her so she could barely draw breath. Their jeans were next. They tugged and grabbed and dragged without any care or finesse. She throbbed with need and from the intense look in his eyes, and the very impressive erection nudging at her, she knew he felt the same. Before she realized what had happened, she was standing naked with him in her own kitchen. The bedroom was too impossibly far, she knew her legs would never carry her there. So she pressed herself against him, kissing his mouth even as she reached down and wrapped her hand around him. He groaned. And then lifting her by her hips hoisted her to the counter. The old laminate felt cool under her hot flesh.

He feasted on her mouth, and then kissed his way down to her breasts. While he lavished his mouth on the sensitive peaks he slipped a hand between her legs. She was so wet, so hot, just his touch on her sensitive flesh had her squirming and moaning. She grabbed his shoulders. "Need you. In me." She managed.

She thought that he scooped up his discarded jeans with his foot and tossed them in the air before grabbing them and digging out a condom. She was happy for his foresight since she did not keep condoms in her apartment. She'd fantasized about being with James and then told herself all the reasons why it would never happen.

"You sure you're ready?" he panted, coming close so that his hardness was pressed against her.

"Oh, I am more than ready," she whispered back.

He did not need any more encouragement. Tightening his grip on her hips he pushed slowly into her. She felt the slow, easy slide, as his body joined with hers. She wrapped her legs around his hips and gave herself over to the sensations as they danced to an ancient rhythm. She ground herself against him, and then she felt her whole body clench around him as fireworks seemed to go off behind her eyelids. Her head fell back as the spasms shook her. In the echo of her own cries she heard him give a heartfelt groan and then shudder as he spilled himself inside her.

As their breath began to head back to normal he said, "I can't believe we didn't even make it to the bedroom."

She looked at him through half closed eyes. "I always do my best work in the kitchen."

CHAPTER 11

*T*he whirring of the industrial mixer kept pace with the beat of her heart as Kim relived that morning again and again.

She tried to focus all her attention on her work but the trouble with being a baker was that once she'd done the tricky part of getting the exact amounts and ingredients right for each recipe, there wasn't a lot of brainpower required. She had machinery that worked efficiently, timers to remind her when to move to the next step.

At least the cookies she'd designed gave her something else to think about besides how James's mouth had felt on her sensitive skin, the expression in his eyes when he'd been deep inside her, the sounds he made. No. Stop!

James had told her there there was a boy and a girl, so she'd had fun with pink and blue icing. Every time she looked at them they made her smile. She'd chosen a very plain sugar cookie recipe, cut out rounds and then once they were baked to perfection she decorated each cookie half in blue icing, half in pink. The top part of the cookie said *It's a Girl* in the bottom part read *It's a Boy*.

She piped tiny rattles and baby buggy shapes onto each one.

As she had suspected, by the time she opened Sunflower, the news was already buzzing that Iris was a mom. Her very first customer was a teacher at Geoff's school. She came up to the counter with a grin. "Good morning. I guess Iris and Geoff are going to be pretty busy now."

"I guess." She whipped up the woman's cappuccino with practiced efficiency, and then pulled out the tray of her special cookies. "Have a cookie to celebrate the birth."

The teacher laughed. "Those are great. I'll happily take one, but you'd better let me buy some for the rest of the staff."

She had already anticipated that this might happen, so she had baked plenty and was soon packing a box of two dozen of her special celebration cookies. The teacher had barely left, the cardboard bakery box swinging from her fingers, when a trio of older ladies walked in.

They were regulars. She said, "Have you heard the news? Iris and Geoff had the twins!"

She had a cookie for each of them to go with their coffees and they settled at a table chatting happily. Group after group began to arrive and by eight in the morning the coffee shop was as packed as she'd ever seen it. It really was like a birthday party she thought as people laughed and giggled and back-slapped. Her cookies were a huge hit and, while not everyone bought extra cookies, it seemed that as soon as she gave something away they felt obliged to buy half a dozen muffins or a couple of lemon dream bars or some brownies to take home.

When James walked in around nine she glanced up and felt herself blush. She only hoped if any of the old busybodies noticed her red cheeks they would assume it was from the heat of the kitchen or the way she was rushing around trying do everything single-handedly.

Before James could reach her, Edna May Tittlebury came forward with a beautifully wrapped package. "I waited until I knew the sex of the babies. This is a little something I'd like you to give Iris for me."

"Sure. I'd be happy to." It was funny the way everyone assumed she and Iris were close friends. She added the package to the growing pile of cards and small gifts that had already accumulated. James greeted Edna May and after the older woman had left, she said, "And what can I get you?" Trying to be very cool and professional.

He sent her a glance that was anything but cool and professional and said, "What do you suggest?"

There was no denying the flirtation in his tone as he said the words. She pulled out the tray of cookies and said, "I recommend one of today's special cookies."

He laughed out loud when he saw them. "I wondered what you had in mind. These are great!" She handed him his cookie on a square of waxed paper and he said, "I guess I'll take an Americano to go with that."

"To go?"

He glanced around at the party atmosphere and said, "No. I'll have it here. Oh, and here's a picture." He handed her a glossy 8X10 of the babies in their tiny pink and blue caps.

"Oh, this is perfect."

"I'll go stick the picture up on the wall while I'm waiting for my coffee."

"Coming right up," she said. Hank Goldberg, who kept bees on his property and sold honey from a roadside stand, sidled up with a brown bag and put it on the counter beside her. "This is a jar of my honey. I made a special label to commemorate the event." He ducked his head shyly. "There's a small jar in there for you, too."

She was so touched. "Why, thank you." She pulled the jar of honey from the bag and he'd designed a label that said, "It's a BEEutiful day to be born," and then the date. "You'll see she gets it?"

"Of course. I know she'll appreciate it. And thanks for including me." He nodded, said, "Remind Iris that babies can't have honey for a year. It's for her and Geoff."

"Of course."

Hank didn't order anything, refused a cookie, and headed out the way he came in. She said to James, "It's funny, people are bringing me things to take to Iris. They ask me questions as though we're close friends."

He shook his head. "Everyone can see that you two like each other. That you're friends."

His words warmed her. "I hope we are."

"And watch that Hank. He obviously has a crush on you."

After their morning's activities she couldn't believe James would think so. "He does not."

"Then why did he rush out of here when he saw me?

He thinks you are BEEutiful."

"No!" She giggled like a schoolgirl.

"He does." He lowered his tone. "And he's right."

She didn't have to answer, as Eric the screenwriter came up to the counter. His computer bag hung from his shoulder. He said, "I heard the good news."

"Yes, isn't it exciting?" She was about to offer him a cookie, when he passed her an envelope, blushing rosily.

"I wrote Iris a poem. I don't usually write poems, but I didn't have time to finish the screenplay. The babies came too early."

"I'm sure she'll love your poem. Thank you." Then she offered him a cookie.

"Hey, those are cool." He glanced around. "But I don't think I'm staying. It's too crowded in here." He did not look as though he approved of a busy, noisy coffee shop. "I need to work. Guess I'll go to the library."

She put one of the cookies in a bag. "Here. For when you take a break."

"Thanks. Guess I might as well take a coffee to go."

While she continued serving up coffees and teas and soy lattes and chai lattes and *It's a Boy!* and *It's a Girl!* cookies, along with all the usual products the coffee shop sold, she kept a casual eye on James. He might pretend to be simply a guy enjoying a coffee break, but she could see the way he worked the room.

Naturally, since he was Iris's brother, he was pelted with questions and congratulations as he moved from group to group. He was very much a presence in this town and she wondered how far that went to deter crime.

Her whole life she'd been taught to run a mile if she saw a cop, but now, instead of wanting to run from James, she wanted to run to him.

She glanced up and suddenly realized the line of people waiting for her services was longer than any line she'd ever seen before at Sunflower. People stood chatting in twos and threes clear outside the door.

Dosana was busy with the other bakery, but had promised to come early and help with the extra baking for the next few days until the excitement over Iris's twins died down. Which was great, but didn't help her right now. She had part-time students arriving but not until school was over. A feeling very much like panic began to beat at her chest when, from the corner of her eye, she saw James come around the side of the bakery case, walk behind her and calmly pick up one of the Sunflower aprons and slip it on over his uniform.

"What are you doing?" She asked him in an urgent under voice.

"My civic duty," he said putting his mouth close to her ear. "I've helped Iris before. Don't worry." And then much louder he said, "What can I get for the next person in line?"

She discovered that James had hidden talents. Not only could he bag a muffin, which any fool could do, but he could run the cash register, and he was reasonably adept on the Barista machine. After five minutes of worrying that he was going to make her job harder, she began to relax knowing she could count on him. The cookies continued to be a huge hit and added to the party atmosphere.

Ralph from the stationary store arrived carrying a bouquet of pink and blue balloons, with two huge ones in the center that said Congratulations On The New Baby.

"Thought they'd be fun in here, and when you close up you can take them home to Iris," he said.

She took the bouquet over to the table where the gifts sat and the balloons bobbed in joyous fashion every time someone new came into the bakery.

As busy as she was, she never lost her intense awareness of James. Close beside her, brushing past her, leaning across the counter to deliver an order—she felt him. Smelled him. All but quivered when he grew close. They touched inadvertently a few times and she felt as though he'd kissed the part he touched.

At one point, he leaned close and said, "I'm going to have to get to work, but how would it be if I call Marguerite in to help? She's not as good as I am, but she's an extra pair of hands."

"Be great," she answered, assuming he wouldn't have suggested his sister if she didn't have bakery experience.

He disappeared into the kitchen and a couple of minutes later emerged. "She's on her way," he said. Then much louder, "Morning, Loreen. What can I get you?"

She glanced up and saw Loreen Ludlow lean as close to James as the bakery counter would allow, and purr at him. "Don't you look good enough to eat in that apron?"

Since she knew from Iris that James did not reciprocate Loreen's obvious interest, she didn't waste her time feeling jealous, but instead intervened to save him embarrassment. When had this started? This feeling that she wanted to make James's life easier? She said, "Loreen, have a special cookie. I baked them myself. I'd love to have your opinion." Then, to James, she said,

"Could you get the next batch of muffins out of the oven? I think I heard the timer go off."

He looked grateful as he headed for the kitchen.

Loreen and she both watched him go. "Doesn't that man just make your insides hum?"

"Oh, yeah."

While she prepared Loreen's skinny latte, the other woman said, "You know, I'm working with the local TV station. I'd love to interview Iris about running a business while she's busy with twin babies. Can you ask her to call me?" She handed Kim a business card.

"I sure will." As Loreen turned away, Kim said, "You didn't take a cookie."

The woman smiled at her. "Can't. The camera adds ten pounds."

She didn't hear a click so much as sensed that she was being photographed. She glanced up in alarm and saw someone she didn't recognize rapidly snapping pictures of her behind the bakery counter. He was a heavyset man and he gave her a nod as he saw her staring at him in horror. Then he turned the camera and took random pictures around the coffee shop. She leaned towards James, who was busy packing a bag with blueberry bran muffins. She said, "James, who was that man? Why is he taking my picture?"

He glanced at her first in surprise and then scanned the place until he identified the photographer. "That's Charlie Mars. He's the Mayor."

"What is he going to do with those pictures?"

"I don't know." He raised his voice, "Charlie, come over here and have one of the special cookies."

The large man obligingly bumbled over, and grinned hugely when he saw the cookies. He raised the camera and snapped a picture of them before she could move her face away. "Well, I don't mind if I do. You the young lady made these?" He held out his hand. "I don't think we've met. I'm Charlie."

She shook his hand and gave him a nervous smile. Beside her, James said, "What's with the photographs Charlie?"

"Thought I'd put a few on the town's Facebook page. Nobody ever seems to read about the town meetings or our new sewer project. I thought this might get some online media engagement."

James nodded. "Great idea. Just make sure you get photo releases for anyone who's appearing in public."

The mayor stared. "Photo releases for a Facebook page?"

She knew James was doing this for her and she was so grateful. He said, without looking at her, "I'm afraid it's the law. If that's a public page, then you'll need photo releases."

"Crap." He took a cookie. "Maybe I'll put a picture of the cookies up, and a long shot of the coffee shop from outside, so you can't identify anyone. That be okay?"

"I think that would be fine. And I'm sure Iris would love copies of the rest. Give her an idea of what she's missing."

When the mayor had left, holding a second cookie, she whispered, "Thanks."

About a quarter of an hour later, Marguerite walked in, and with her was her fiancé, Alexei. While Marguerite got stopped by every other person who wanted to hear the latest on Iris and the twins, Alexei, the gorgeous Greek God of Food Trucks, came behind the counter and took James's apron.

"Can you work the Barista machine?" Kim asked him.

He spread his hands. "Did the Greeks invent the Olympic games?"

"Is that a yes?"

He grinned at her and she thought he could serve anything he liked when he looked at a woman that way. "It's a yes."

While Alexei cheerfully served the next customer, James said, "Could I see you in the kitchen for a moment?"

"Of course." Mystified, she followed him into the kitchen. "What is—"

He kissed her long and hard. "I've been thinking about doing that since I left your place this morning."

She sighed, leaned into him for one more kiss. "Me, too."

"Can I see you tonight?"

She hesitated. There was nothing she wanted more, but if she started seeing him regularly, where would it lead? "I...I'm going to visit Iris after we close. Then, I'm not sure."

He looked as though he was going to say more, but Marguerite walked in at that moment. "Are there any more baby cookies?"

She busied herself with cookies, and James said, "I'll see you both later," sent her a look that said, as clear as words, 'this is not over' and let himself out the kitchen door.

CHAPTER 12

Three mornings later, Kimberly walked into the kitchen of Sunflower stifling a yawn. It was four in the morning. The lights were already on, which meant Dosana was there before her. For the past three nights she'd slept poorly, mostly because she yearned for James in the night almost as actively as she avoided him in the day.

She was in an impossible situation and had no idea what to do.

"Morning," she said, feeling tired and groggy.

Even through her morning stupor she sensed something was wrong. Dosana stood beside the bread oven like a stone statue. "Dosana?"

"Don't make any sudden moves," the woman said, not even turning her head. She sounded tense, frightened. Immediately, the last wisps of fatigue cleared as she stepped slowly forward. "What's going on?"

She couldn't immediately see any broken machinery. Or smell anything, like smoke. Nothing that would account for Dosana's peculiar attitude.

Until she stood beside Dosana, following the woman's fixed

gaze. Then she immediately understood the reason for her standing frozen in shock.

A snake was coiled in front of the oven. It wasn't a small snake, either. Not one of those little garden snakes that occasionally skittered away when she crossed a gravel path. This was a large snake. A very large snake.

It looked like the kind of snake that would emerge from a snake charmer's wicker basket and do some kind of terrifying dance. "What do we do?" Dosana asked in a whisper.

"I have no idea. How long has it been there?"

"I don't know. It was here when I arrived. I'm scared to move. See the way he's staring at me? He's licking his lips in anticipation."

"I don't think snakes have lips." But she could see the tongue flicking in and out too.

"Is it poisonous?"

"I don't know much about reptiles."

They both stood staring at the snake. It stared back with tiny black eyes. It was curled into a mound of brown and green and gray and its tongue continued to flick out from time to time. While they watched, the snake moved, stretching its head toward them. Dosana gave a squeak of alarm and jumped back. "I'm so scared."

Kim could see the powerful muscles ripple as it shifted but it only seemed to be curling into a more comfortable position. "I think maybe it just wanted to get warmed by the stove."

"But it can't stay here!"

"I know. What do you suggest we do?"

"Call the sheriff."

She glanced over at Dosana. "The sheriff? What do you want him to do? Arrest it?"

Dosana shook her head, barely moving. "He can shoot it."

She stared at the snake. The snake stared back. While she wasn't thrilled to have a large reptile curled up in the kitchen of the bakery, it seemed unnecessary to shoot the poor thing. Still, she didn't have a better idea than to call James. He seemed like a sensible person, the kind that you could call at four the morning when you were trapped in the kitchen with a dangerous animal.

In fact, she'd wanted to call him all night.

She slowly stepped back keeping her eyes fixed on the snake but it merely watched her retreat without attempting to follow, bite or strangle her, which seemed like a good thing.

She grabbed her cell phone from her bag. Found James's number in her contacts and called. He probably wouldn't even answer at this hour. But, on the second ring, he said "Sheriff Chance," in a surprisingly strong voice.

"Sheriff, I'm really sorry to bother you, but—"

"Kim?" He sounded wide-awake now. "Are you in trouble?"

She was so grateful that he had answered the phone. "We have a, um, situation at the bakery."

"What is it? An intruder?" His tone sharpened. She heard rustling and pictured him grabbing his uniform, dressing rapidly as he talked. She stifled a hysterical giggle. "Sort of. Yes. It is an intruder. But not human."

His tone sharpened. "What do you mean, not human?"

"It's a snake. A very large snake. I don't know what kind, but maybe a boa constrictor?" She'd seen them on TV and once in a zoo. "It's in the kitchen and it's got me and Dosana trapped here."

Dosana cried out, "It moved! I think I might faint."

"Don't faint!" she commanded.

In her ear James said, "Stay where you are. Do not move. I'm coming right over."

"Just please don't shoot it."

IN MINUTES she heard the blessed sound of a car pulling up outside the bakery. A car door slammed. She said softly to Dosana, "Do you want to go and let him in?" Because of course she'd locked the door behind her when she entered the premises this morning. They couldn't use the kitchen door since the snake was there. Dosana said, "I can't move."

"Okay, don't panic. The sheriff's here. I'm pretty sure it's a constrictor and they're not poisonous." She wasn't at all sure if that was true but she didn't want Dosana fainting or in any other way upsetting their serpentine morning visitor. If she recalled correctly, the boa constrictor wrapped itself around its victim before squeezing it to death. She did not share this information with Dosana.

She backed out of the kitchen slowly and then ran to the door where James was standing. He wore the slightly stunned expression of someone up too early but he was completely alert and when he saw her he gave her a reassuring smile. "You okay?"

She nodded, relieved now that he was here, believing somehow that he could solve this problem or at least make it go away. As he stepped inside she noticed he had a laundry hamper and a burlap sack in his hand. She glanced at him, puzzled. He shrugged. "It was all I had handy."

She led the way and he followed. When he got to the kitchen he said, in a very calm voice, "Dosana, I'm going to come and stand beside you, and when I get there, I want you to take a step backwards. A nice slow one and then another one until you're out of the kitchen. Can you do that?"

He was going to put himself between Dosana and the snake.

Dosana nodded stiffly. "I'm allergic to wasp stings," she said, as though that was relevant.

James nodded, as if that was a perfectly normal reaction to facing a boa constrictor and said, "Okay. I'll make sure it doesn't bite you. It probably just came in to warm up by the oven." His voice was so soothing, she could see Dosana's rigid shoulders begin to relax and ease away from her ears. She took one step back. Then a second step. And then she kept going until she was all the way out of the kitchen. "I'll set up out front," she announced. She'd arrived early to help bake, but Kim understood that she hadn't counted on a large reptile in the kitchen, and even setting things up out front would be a help.

Kim might not be the bravest woman in the world, but she didn't want to leave James here. Maybe he needed help snake wrangling. He took a step toward the snake. Once more it shifted and they were treated to a demonstration of the way the powerful muscles rippled. "You have any experience with snakes?" he asked her.

"No. You?"

"No."

She said, "Couldn't we barricade it in here and call a zoo or something."

He shook his head. "I don't want it getting out and terrorizing anybody else." To her surprise, he pulled out his cell phone, fiddled with the focus and took a close up of the snake.

"Would you like me to snap the two of you together?"

"I'm sending a photo to my sister. Lauren's a vet. Maybe she can ID the snake."

Slowly he stepped towards the snake which began to rock back and forth as though it were listening to a funky tune. James took another step forward. Her heart was pounding. She didn't know what she'd do if it attacked him.

"I'm not going to hurt you," he said quietly to the snake. The snake did not look convinced.

She grabbed a heavy frying pan. She thought if it made a move on James she might be able to run in and hit it on the head or something. If she had to. Maybe.

He took another step forward. "What are you doing?" she squeaked.

"Think about it. This did not come in from the wild. There isn't a zoo for miles. It has to be a pet. It seems pretty accustomed to humans."

She tightened her grip on the skillet and held her breath as

James eased the hamper down and over the snake's head and body. The snake moved its head and body as though unsure about the hamper but it didn't slither away and in no time, James had it contained.

She returned the pan to its hook on the wall and it made a rattling sound.

James said, "Can you pass me one of those cookie sheets?"

"Sure." She passed him one of their flat stainless steel industrial cookie sheets. It was much larger than the mouth of the basket but still she thought it was the bravest thing she'd ever seen when James slid the cookie sheet underneath the wicker basket. He talked to the snake, the way she might've spoken to a child frightened by a dog. Soothing, slow, as he leaned over to ease the pan under the basket she watched the powerful muscles of his shoulders and back moving under his uniform shirt.

Her mouth went dry at the sheer beauty of the man in his everyday bravery.

"Okay. We've got it contained." He glanced up her, keeping his hand on the top of the basket. "Now what the hell do I do with it?"

She was wondering the same thing. "Your sister didn't get back to you?"

"No. She probably has her phone off."

"Well, as you said, he escaped from somewhere. Is there a pet store? Or somebody who raises reptiles locally?"

He shook his head, "Not that I know of. I can only think of one person to call," he said and took a step toward her.

"Should you really walk away from the snake?"

"No. You better make the call." He resumed his position with his hand firmly on top of the laundry hamper. Through the holes she could see the snake sitting there staring back at her.

She picked up her phone. He said, "Call my dad. If anybody knows what's going on around here, it will be him."

She glanced at the time on her cell. "It's four forty-five in the morning."

"He's an early riser."

He recited the number and she punched it in. The phone only rang once and was picked up. A cheerful voice said, "Jack Chance speaking. It's a beautiful morning."

A little of her tension eased. "It is, Mr. Chance. This is Kimberly calling From Sunflower Coffee and Tea Company."

His voice sharpened. "Is it Iris? Is she okay?"

"Oh, yes, everything's fine. I'm not calling about Iris. I've got your son James here."

"James? What's he doing at the bakery at five in the morning?"

"Well, there's a big snake in the kitchen. We think it's a boa constrictor."

"A boa? Where is it now?"

"In a laundry hamper."

"How the hell did a snake crawl into a laundry hamper in a bakery kitchen?"

James was giving her the *move along* signal with his free hand. She said, "James has trapped it in the laundry hamper. Mr. Chance, we're wondering if you have any idea who the snake might belong to?"

"My best guess is to call Enid Parkinson."

"Does the snake belong to her?"

"I don't know. Does it answer to the name of Alice?"

"Alice?"

"Who's Alice," James asked, looking confused.

"The snake. Who calls a huge snake Alice?"

It did seem as though the reptile head moved whenever she repeated the name.

Into the phone she said, "It seems to respond to Alice. Would you have the owner's number?"

She couldn't imagine that Jack and Daphne would have the phone number of a person who not only owned an enormous snake, but named it Alice, but he said, "Sure I do, somewhere." She could hear him moving around, shuffling papers and then some wood on wood banging, as though he were opening cupboards or drawers. "I think she's on the phone tree."

She heard a bang and then, "Sorry, I dropped the phone. I don't want to wake Daphne, but she's the one who knows where the phone numbers are. Oh, this looks like a telephone book. Yep, here we go. Wait a minute, is that an eight or a zero? Or maybe a three? Hang on, honey. I'll get my glasses."

She had visions of phoning three different people at five in the morning asking if they owned the snake. She wished she'd stayed in bed with the covers over her head.

James said, "What is going on?"

"He has to find his glasses."

James nodded, looking frustrated, and they both waited. In another minute she had Jack back on the phone. "Okay, I got my glasses. Now let's see, yes, here it is. Okay it wasn't a zero or an eight. It was a three. He gave her the number. She repeated it to be certain she had all the digits correct and then, thanking him, disconnected.

"Do you want me to call this woman?" she asked James.

"You can do that or you can babysit the snake."

"I'll make the call."

CHAPTER 13

Once more she heard a phone ringing. It rang about seven times before an older woman's voice said. "Hello?"

She felt terrible waking an old woman so early in the morning. "Is this Enid Parkinson?"

"This is she. How may I help you?"

"I am so sorry to bother you so early, but are you by any chance missing a snake?"

"Alice! Have you found her?"

"Is Alice a very large snake with brown and gray and green markings?"

"Yes, that sounds exactly like her." The woman sounded delighted. "Wait until I get my hands on my little girl."

"If you could come quite soon, that would be great. Do you know where the Sunflower Coffee and Tea Company is?"

"Of course I do, dear. In fact, if it wasn't so early, I'd ask you to make me a pot of your lovely English breakfast tea. It's the best tea I've had outside of England."

"I'm so glad you like our tea." She widened her eyes to James who was pointing at the snake and then at himself.

"Not just the tea. I think your baking is excellent. I'm particularly partial to the lemon dream bars. Although, I can't eat too many, I have to watch my sugar intake."

"So, we'll see you in a few minutes?"

"Yes, I'll get dressed and be right down."

She hung up and said to James. "She's very partial to our lemon dream bars."

"I should lock that woman up and throw away the key."

"Don't do that. Who's going to look after Alice?"

"Alice? She really named a snake Alice?"

"I think so." She glanced at the clock and saw that she'd wasted all the extra time she'd given herself for the baking, and more. "Do you mind if I start baking? We're way behind."

"Don't mind me. Alice and I are happy to watch you work."

She felt a little self-conscious doing the morning baking in front of James. Normally she worked alone, or if there were multiple bakers, everybody was measuring flour, rolling pastry, icing, mixing, passing back and forth behind each other to get to the ovens. It was strange to have this immobile and very sexy man with nothing better to do than watch her.

And talk to her. "I missed you last night," he said.

She dropped the stainless steel flour scoop so it clattered to the worktop. "That's nice."

"I missed you the night before, too. In fact, I miss you a lot."

She heard the sincerity behind his words and confusion as though he was wondering why she had avoided him since that amazing session in her apartment kitchen. "I didn't hurt you, did I?"

"No. Oh, no." She wanted to tell him that was the best sex she'd ever had, but then he'd want to know why they weren't having more of it. "I've been busy, that's all. With Iris home and the bakery so busy…"

He didn't push the issue, merely stood quietly while she worked.

She felt a strange urge to tell him what she was doing, as

though she were offering him a cooking course on television. She bit back the impulse, trying to focus on making sure she made the recipe correctly. She was so flustered between the snake and the man she was certain she was going to goof up somehow.

She had just finished putting the first tray of muffins into the oven when she heard the chimes of the front door and voices out front. A moment later a tiny woman with corkscrews of gray hair dressed in a royal blue jogging suit entered the kitchen. Kim noticed that she hadn't left her house without applying pink lipstick. When she saw Kimberly, she said, "You must be the girl who called me. Thank you so much, dear. I hope Alice hasn't been any trouble."

James spoke from the corner in a tone Kim had never heard him use before. He was all tough cop. "Alice has been a world of trouble. She terrorized these two poor women when they came into the bakery this morning."

Enid Parkinson put a hand to her chest. "Oh my goodness. Sheriff Chance. I'm so very sorry that you should be bothered." She glanced at the basket. "May I see her?"

"I was hoping we could transport her in the basket.

She shook her head so her curls danced. "Oh my goodness, that won't be necessary. Alice has been my dear friend for ten years. She walked forward.

With a glance at Kimberly and a slight shrug, he slowly lifted basket off the snake. She felt her breath hitch for a moment as once more the coiled serpent was before her. The lady bent over and said, "What do you have to say for yourself you naughty girl?"

It was astonishing but the snake moved towards the sound of the woman's voice. She reached out and stroked the sinewy body and then before Kim's horrified gaze she picked up the snake, handling it as though it were a child. The snake began to wrap itself around her. For a moment Kim had a terrible vision of it wrapping around the woman's neck and squeezing the life out of her, but it merely settled itself around her shoulders like a snake-skin shawl.

"Alice is a carpet python."

"Still deadly, I'm guessing."

"Well, to a small rodent, perhaps. But not to a human. We're too big, you see."

"That's a relief."

"I'm very sorry to cause so much trouble. I left her sitting in the window. She likes to sun herself and see what's going on outside. I must have forgotten to put her back into her tank and the little monkey slipped out the cat door."

"You have cats?" Kimberly asked.

The woman with the cherubic cheeks smiled at her serenely, "Not anymore."

"Did Alice…?" She couldn't even finish the sentence.

The woman laughed merrily. "Of course not. The cats died of old age. Anyway, she doesn't eat anything that large. She likes a nice mouse. Oh, I don't have mice in my house, I buy them from the pet store. It is a bit gruesome at first, but you get used to it. And she's a lovely companion." She stroked the snake's neck as she spoke. "I'll take her straight home and I'll make sure she doesn't get out again."

"You do that," James said. And the pair of them watched as the woman walked out chattering away to the snake.

When the bells jingled again to signal Alice's departure, she let out a sigh of relief. James picked up the laundry hamper. Glanced at it. "Doing my laundry will never be the same."

"Thank you," There didn't seem to be any more she could say that wouldn't sound trite.

"Only doing my job." Then he assessed her progress. "I'll let you get back to baking." And he was gone.

Well, snake invasion or not, they still had to get Sunflower open in time to greet the early birds, preferably with some of the baking that drew not only residents, but commuters who veered off I-5 on a regular basis for their morning fix. By working flat out, Kim and Dosana managed to get enough baking in the oven that the crisis of an empty bakery case was averted.

She thought about James as she worked. She thought about what he had said. "Only doing my job." She knew there was a darkness to his former work in Seattle that cast a shadow. She understood that this young, vital man had chosen to become a sheriff in Hidden Falls for that very reason. He probably liked the fact that nothing much ever happened here. In a way, he was a refugee from a harsher world like she was. She'd been running one way or another since she'd left Nelson.

She was tired of running. She began to wonder, what if? What if she told a law enforcement officer, a sheriff, about her past? Would he have her deported? Jailed? Worst of all, would they force her to testify against her father? Of all the possible evils of her situation, testifying against her father was the worse. It wasn't that she wanted to protect her dad so much, it was her mom and siblings she worried about. He talked about retiring but never had. He'd become too addicted to the easy money.

She wondered what the chances were that she and James could have a successful relationship and decided they were small to none. Still, she made time to put six of the most perfect of his favorite muffins into a bag. As Dosana was heading out, she said, "Can you drop this off at the sheriff's on your way to the other bakery? It's a thank you for Sheriff Chance."

"What a great idea." Dosana took the gesture a step farther by retrieving one of the special cards Iris had had printed on recycled card stock with the Sunflower logo. Dosana, who'd recovered her good humor now the snake was gone, wrote in her big, loopy handwriting, "Thanks, Sheriff, for saving two damsels in distress."

Kim smiled when she read the younger woman's inscription. She simply added a "Thank you. Kim", in her own much less exuberant writing.

"Okay, gotta run," Dosana said, grabbing the muffins and card and heading out with a wave. She got to the door and then turned and said, "Oh, by the way, next time I help with baking you have to get here first." The jingle of sunflower bells joined with Kim's laughter and Dosana was gone.

JAMES WALKED into the meeting room in the library, which was separated only by a wall from City Hall where his own offices were. It was a couple of minutes before the meeting about the Fourth of July celebrations began and he heard chatter coming from the boardroom long before he got there.

He was a couple of minutes ahead of the start time and still the last to arrive. He liked to see that sense of dedication in his committee members. Edna May and Harold were chatting like old pals. He caught what sounded like 'fife and drums.' Loreen was talking to his mom and it was all about the kitten Loreen had adopted from Lauren. "It's the cutest little thing I've ever seen. I know I shouldn't, but I let it sleep on the bed with me."

Better the kitten, he thought, than her trying to get him as her bed partner.

No one even noticed him so he took a minute to settle himself at the head of the boardroom table, pull out the file folder his predecessor had left and click open a ball point pen which he laid on top of the blank pad of paper before him. "Okay, folks, I call this meeting to order."

James glanced around. One thing you could say about this committee, they weren't a quiet bunch—they were still chatting and gossiping. This was the same room where the town council held its meetings, so he grabbed the Mayor's gavel and banged it sharply. That got their attention. They took seats around the table and all stared at him.

In the sudden silence, he said again, "I call this meeting to order."

James wasn't big on formality, but sometimes it really helped keep things moving. He said, "Edna May, can I ask you to take notes and act as secretary for tonight's meeting?"

She blushed with pleasure. "Certainly, Sheriff, I'd be happy to." He glanced around his committee. I think we all know each other, but let's go around and introduce ourselves anyway. We'll start with you, Harold."

The older man beamed." I'm Harold Biedleman." Harold was a retiree who had relocated to Oregon to escape the harsh winters Back East where he'd spent most of his life. He had a booming Boston-accented voice. He said, "I wanted to get involved in something interesting and help support my town, so here I am."

"Welcome. Loreen?"

Loreen had chosen to wear a clinging, low cut black top, and he noticed that Harold's eyes darted to her impressive cleavage as she introduced herself. "I'm Loreen Ludlow and the Sheriff asked me specially to take part in this committee." She glanced at him from under her eyelashes as though he might have said the words to her from across the pillow. "And since I'm also working for the local TV station, I thought I'd volunteer myself as media liaison."

"Excellent. Thank you, Loreen." And he raised his brows at Edna May. She put down her pen.

"I'm Edna May Tittlebury," she said. "I've lived in this town all my life and I am here to make sure that we uphold the noble traditions of Hidden Falls. Our Fourth of July celebrations have always been a real highlight of our town's social calendar. I'm going to do everything I can to make sure that continues."

"Thank you Edna May. Daphne?"

His mother twinkled at them all. "I'm Daphne Chance. I'm excited to help make this year's festivities the best ever."

"Wonderful." He continued around the table. There were four other committee members there, all community-minded citizens he felt he could trust. All of them had served on the Fourth of July committee at least once before.

"Okay, everybody," James said opening the file before him. He'd glanced at it earlier, and he felt sure that he and his committee could follow the same format without too much trouble.

"I've got the schedule of events from last year." He passed copies around the table. "I thought we'd run through the schedule and see if we want to amend it in any way, otherwise, we'll go ahead and order the same fireworks." They went through the list of attractions that had been part of the event every year. "In the morning, we've got the 5K fun run, followed by a pancake break-fast. Then the family fun fair, with balloon animals, a petting zoo, a few games and music. Last year we had a climbing wall and a bouncy castle. Do we want those again?"

"Oh, yes," Daphne said. "I missed out on the climbing wall and I definitely want to try it."

He'd kind of imagined the climbing wall was for kids, but he kept his mouth shut.

"Before we start deciding who's in charge of what, does anybody have any questions or additions or suggestions?"

Harold spoke up. "I've got a suggestion. I think we should do a Revolutionary War reenactment."

James stared at him feeling his jaw go slack. "A Revolutionary War reenactment?"

CHAPTER 14

*J*ames wasn't the only person on the committee staring at Harold, who seemed unfazed by the surprised reactions. "Absolutely. We celebrate the Fourth of July as our Independence Day. But I am surprised at how few of the young people in this town really understand what went on in those battles. I propose that we give them a taste of what our freedom cost."

He glanced at Frank Zolman, a history teacher at the high school whose eyes had widened slightly at the suggestion. He cleared his throat and said, "But, Harold, we didn't fight any revolutionary battles here in Oregon."

"I'm aware of that, Frank. But I feel that no matter where we are in this great nation of ours we should celebrate the Founding Fathers and the founding battles."

Frank said, "Wouldn't we need more people?"

Harold beamed at him as though he were a student who'd asked the right question, instead of a teacher. "Yes indeed. I've taken care of that. I go to a reenactment every year in Ohio. I have already broached the topic and they'd be more than happy to come along."

Vaguely, James had a feeling this was a very bad idea. His simple Fourth of July parade and fireworks seemed like it was going to turn into a Revolutionary War battle if he didn't do something right now to nip this idea in the bud. Even as he opened his mouth to do that Edna May Tittlebury beamed at Harold. "I have to say, Harold, that I think this is a wonderful idea. I'd be happy to help with uniforms to make sure that the historical accuracy is as good as it can be, and naturally, I will wear a historical costume." She glanced up at Harold in a manner that could only be termed flirtatious. "It may interest you to know that one of my ancestors fought at Bunker Hill."

Loreen glanced at Harold in an appraising way. She said, "The soldiers who will be coming to Hidden Falls, are they all retired like you?"

He chuckled. "No indeed. I'm one of the oldest. Why they are schoolteachers and historians and the members of gun clubs. You'd be amazed at the people who take part. I can guarantee you it will put Hidden Falls on the map."

"I can get my students involved for class credit," Frank said, clearly warming up to the idea.

He glanced in appeal to Daphne. His mother was a pacifist if there ever was one. She said, "Well, we've never done anything like this before. I bet it would bring more folks out. Really get the community together. What do you think, James?"

"I think we should do some research on this, and table it for the next meeting." During which time he hoped to talk everyone involved out of this crazy idea.

But Harold gave him a knowing look as though being perfectly aware what he was up to. He said, "I think we should take a vote now. We haven't got much time until July. If I'm going to get my buddies committed, I need to make calls. Send emails."

And before you could say *this meeting is adjourned*, they'd taken a vote and passed the resolution.

He was about to leave the meeting, a lot less confident of how easy it would be to plan this celebration than when the meeting had started, when his mom pulled him to one side. She waited until everyone had left the room and said, "I have to admit, I thought you'd lost your mind asking Edna May and Loreen to sit on the committee, but you know, it was a good idea. I thought tonight's meeting went really well. A reenactment, that should be fun."

"I don't know, Mom. Having a bunch of old geezers playing war games seems like it could go wrong."

"Nonsense." She smiled at him. "We have a great sheriff. He'll keep everyone in line."

"I was hoping you'd speak out against the idea. I gave you a sign."

"Is that why you were rolling your eyes and twitching your nose? I thought you were trying not to sneeze."

"Remind me never to play poker with you."

She patted his arm. "Can you stop by Iris's tonight?"

He blinked at the sudden change in subject. "Iris? Isn't she busy with the babies?"

"Honestly, I think she's too busy. I'm not sure how well she's managing. I've been dropping by as much as I can, but she'll start thinking I don't trust her mothering skills if I show up too often."

"What do you think I can do? I'm scared to touch those tiny things in case I drop one and break it."

"You can fetch and carry for her, make her some tea and, yes, hold a niece or nephew if they're both screaming at once."

He stared. "They do that?"

"Frequently. When you and Josh used to get going it took me and Iris, who was always good with kids, to calm you down." She smiled at him sweetly. "Seems only fair that you should help her. She helped when you were a screaming baby."

"You don't fight fair, Mom."

She chuckled. "When you've had eleven kids, you won't either."

Oh, like that was ever going to happen. But he did love his sister and if she needed support, he supposed he could help out for an hour. "Okay, I'll head over there. But what do I use as an excuse? We don't have a 'dropping by' relationship, except, obviously when I go to Sunflower for coffee."

She opened a large macramé bag that looked as though it had been made by the blind. Knowing his mom, it probably had. From this lumpy collection of holes she withdrew a wrapped package. "The women at my yoga class got together and bought her a gift. You can use that as an excuse."

"Iris knows I don't do yoga."

"Sometimes I think you're too honest for your own good! Tell her they dropped it off at the station because I wasn't in yoga class today." She tapped his chest. "Little white lie."

"It starts as a little white lie, and next thing I know, I'm visiting you in jail." But he took the package anyway. A glance at his watch told him it was eight o'clock. He headed straight to his sister's.

When he got to Iris's house, he didn't want to ring the bell and stir up sleeping infants. In fact, before doing anything, he stood perfectly still with his ear pressed to the front door listening for any sounds of wailing. Everything seemed quiet. He turned the handle and, as he'd expected, the door opened. He still wasn't accustomed to the way people didn't lock their doors here, which was weird, since he'd grown up in Hidden Falls. But a few years in Seattle had changed his perspective.

He stepped into the hallway. Paused to listen and all was peaceful. He'd heard that young mothers often napped when the babies did, and that had to be doubly true with twins, so he trod soundlessly down the hallway, thinking that if Iris was sleeping he'd simply drop off the package and leave as quietly as he had come. He reached the doorway to the kitchen and stepped inside.

And his heart flipped over.

It wasn't Iris sitting in a reclining chair in the den off the kitchen. To his surprise, it was Kimberly. She looked beautiful and peaceful, Madonna-like, with one tiny infant over one shoulder and the second draped over her other shoulder. They both had their heads turned towards her and their bodies curled inward, settling into her, like quotation marks.

He was scared to even go near them, but she glanced up and gave a start when he entered the kitchen. One of the little babies jerked, its hand opening from where it had been wrapped around a lock of her hair and she made a soothing, shushing sound until the tiny hand closed again around her hair.

"What are you doing here?" He asked so softly he could barely hear the words himself.

She smiled ever so slightly, once more reminding him of the Madonnas that the old masters loved to paint.

"Babysitting," she said. "Iris and Geoff needed to go shopping and so I volunteered to look after the little ones."

"Wow! You're brave."

"I'm really not. I have a lot of experience with babies. And, as you can see, they're no trouble."

He thought about what his mom had said about them wailing in stereo, and he couldn't imagine being this calm if he had to look after such tiny human beings. "What if they get hungry?" According to Iris, they were always hungry.

"I came right after they were fed, and Iris expressed milk, so I can feed them if I need to."

He wished he hadn't asked. He had no idea what expressed milk was and didn't want to find out. He waved the wrapped package. "I brought a gift from the yoga women."

At her skeptical expression, he said, "I know. It was Mom's idea. She didn't want Iris to think she was dropping by too often, so she decided I should do it. But I don't want to disturb you. I should probably get going."

"Do you think you could stay and talk to me for a few minutes? I can't read or watch TV or do anything at the moment."

"Right." He could see that she was trapped there and he was delighted that she wanted to talk to him. "Do you want to hear about the July 4th committee meeting?"

Her eyes began to twinkle. "You know I do."

He laughed. "You're turning into a regular Hidden Fallsian. You know that, right?"

"It's hard not to get involved. The bakery is like gossip central. Everything happens there."

"Really? Like what?" He had his own ideas about what happened in the bakery but he was curious to see how Kim saw things.

She made a movement that was like a shrug without actually moving her shoulders, which would've shifted the babies. "People are lonely sometimes and like to talk, or they're study-ing." Her lips turned up in a secret smile, "Some people fall in love there."

"Fall in love? Who?"

She shook her head. "I don't want to say. And maybe I'm wrong."

"Now I'm intrigued. I'm trying to imagine who it could be." The only person he knew who seemed to be suffering unrequited love was him. The recipient of all that unrequited feeling currently had babies draped all over her like shawls. Their gazes connected and, as though she had read his thoughts, her cheeks pinkened ever so slightly.

After a tiny pause, she said, "You promised to tell me about the meeting." And since when did civic politics trump love? But he went along with her desire to change the subject.

"Well, I figured we'd follow the playbook. Put on the same event we've put on every year for pretty much forever. The old sheriff left notes. Seemed pretty straightforward. But no. Not this year. This year, Harold Biedleman thinks we should stage a Revolutionary War reenactment."

Her nose wrinkled. "I'm Canadian, so excuse me if my history knowledge is fuzzy, but did you fight a Revolutionary War in Oregon?"

"It's not *your* history that's off. It's Harold's. And did Loreen Ludlow argue against this terrible idea, since she's supposed to be about doing something new and modern? No she did not." He thought about the way that meeting had taken off like a riderless horse. "She found out that there are men of all ages who take part in these things and decided she was a hundred percent in favor."

"Oh, dear."

"And then Edna May Tittlebury, who I personally selected for the committee knowing she's a stickler for tradition, figuring she'd never let any funny business into our Fourth of July festivities, lit up like it was Christmas and her birthday wrapped into one. Turns out she had a distant, long-dead relative who fought at Bunker Hill. And she's sewing a costume. She and Harold are going to make sure of the historical accuracy." At her gurgle of laughter, he turned and at the expression on her face, realized what a spectacularly bad detective he was. "It's them, isn't it? The ones falling in love over coffee and banana bread at Sunflower?"

"I think so."

"No wonder I got no support from Edna May."

"But what about your mother? Daphne hates guns. I've heard her rant about them."

"Thank you. My mother, the one person I thought I could count on, thought it was a great idea for a bunch of grown men to dress in regimentals and shout orders and shoot guns."

"Well. Look on the bright side. You've got lots of volunteers. I'm sure it won't be as bad as you think."

But he couldn't rid himself of a feeling of dread.

"So, when do you get off this babysitting gig?"

She shot him a mischievous look. "Why do you ask?"

He thought back to high school when he'd dated girls who babysat. He said, "If you've finished your homework and there's time before your curfew, I thought we'd take a walk. Or a drive."

As though she'd read his mind, Kim opened her eyes wide. "And if I go with you for a walk or a drive, will you behave yourself?"

He couldn't help the grin that spread all over his face. "What do you consider behaving myself? Would, say first base, be okay?"

Her lips twitched. "I am not a baseball diamond."

"Right. And being Canadian and all, I guess you probably don't know the terminology. First base means I want to kiss you."

Her saw her chest rise rapidly as though she'd sucked in a quick breath. One of the twins shifted. "Kissing," she said softly. "I think that would be all right."

"But you know what kissing leads to?"

She stared at him.

He held up his hands as though they were out of his control. "I'm going to want to put my hands somewhere."

"In your pockets?"

"Ouch, that's harsh. I was thinking about second base. That, for someone like yourself, who's from North of the 49th parallel, would be putting my hands under your shirt."

It was crazy to feel himself getting so aroused from such a stupid conversation. He'd only meant to tease her gently, not make himself crazed with wanting her. Even now his palms tingled to have her small breasts in his hands. He knew what she liked, the sounds she made when he caressed her heated flesh.

Her face might remain prim, but her eyes were telling him she was as turned on as he was. "Where exactly, under my shirt, are we talking?"

"Well, naturally, I wouldn't want to rush anything. I'd probably lift the hem of that pretty white shirt from where it's tucked into your jeans." He'd walk over to her and demonstrate if she didn't have two very effective chastity belts, one draped over each shoulder. Not being able to touch her only added to his excitement.

She seemed to enjoy this slow teasing, also. She said, "You think I'd let you untuck my shirt?"

"Not without a lot of kissing first, to warm you up." He had to control himself from getting up right now and going over to kiss her, babies and all. He could practically feel her lips beneath his, taste her, smell her.

"I would need a lot of warming up," she agreed.

"Then, when I had your shirt untucked, I'd slip my hand underneath, touch the warm skin of your belly." His hand twitched in memory. "Do you know how much I like your belly?"

She seemed surprised. "You do?"

"Oh, yeah. It's got tone, but there's also a nice roundness to it. And when I run my hand across your stomach, sometimes you shiver."

"Maybe your hands are cold."

"Maybe you're just hot."

She licked her lips. "So, you're going to all that trouble, untucking my clothing, so you can reach my stomach?"

"Oh, no. That's only the beginning. Thing is, when a guy knows a girl will only go so far, he paces himself. So, I'll spend quite a bit of time on your belly. Then I'll start moving north. You know all about North, being a Canadian."

He saw her try and stifle a giggle. God, he liked her like this, relaxed and sexy.

"I'm guessing I'll hit a barrier."

"The Canadian border?"

"Your bra. In my experience, most babysitters wear them."

"Ah."

"I'd feel you through your bra, maybe squeeze a little, until we were both huffing and puffing."

"I do not huff and puff."

He thought back to their recent time together. Gave her a knowing look. "Yeah, you do."

"Not as much as you do. But go on. Once you've got me

huffing and puffing, even though I'm still wearing all my underwear, then what?"

She might sound prim, but her voice was soft, sweet, liquid, like maple syrup.

"Why then, I reach around your back and release the clasp of your bra."

"I remember you being really smooth at that."

"I dated a lot of babysitters," he admitted.

"You should make sure and add that talent to your online dating profile."

As if he had one, with her clouding his mind and taking up so much of his energy. "Now, when I've got your bra unhooked, you know what I'm going to do?"

"Does it have anything to do with baseball?"

He chuckled. "We're still on second base."

"Baseball is a very slow game."

"Only when it's played right." He leaned forward. "Are you feeling okay? You look a little flushed."

"It's the babies," she lied.

If there was one thing he loved about her it was the way her fair skin blushed when she was embarrassed. Or aroused. That complexion told him all kinds of things. Like the way she was as excited by this silliness as he was.

She looked like a Madonna, with twin cherubs sleeping curled up at her breast, but he could feel the heat of a very sexual woman coming off her.

"Now, where was I?"

"Stalled on second base, I believe."

"Not stalled. Sometimes as part of an overall strategy, a player takes his time. So, I've got your bra undone. Now I slowly reach around, slip my hand under the loosened fabric and close my hand over your naked breast."

"Oh."

"Oh?"

"Just, Oh."

He liked the way her 'oh' sounded. Breathy and eager. Truth was, he was feeling pretty breathy and eager himself.

He could picture them in that very pose. His hand closing over her breast, the way she'd move against him, how her breathing would change. "Of course, I'm not going to simply grab it, like I've got rigor mortis. I'm going to move it around a little."

"Move it around?"

"Caress you."

"Oh." Again with the *oh*.

"Feel your nipple harden against my palm." Those wee babies were as good as an electric fence at keeping him from showing her exactly what he'd do. "I'd spend a lot of time playing with your breasts, but I'd still be kissing you of course."

"You'd be on both bases at once?"

"I'm a very versatile baseball player."

"I can see that."

"Naturally, a player on second always has third base in his sights."

"Third base?"

He was fairly certain they did the same things in Canada. She was toying with him as much as he was with her. "Oh, yeah. You've heard the term 'stealing a base?'"

"I believe I have."

"I'd probably make a stealth move. Keep you so busy with the kissing and playing with your breasts, that I could slip down south, back across the border."

"The border?"

"The waistband of your jeans."

She put on a prudish expression. "You mean?"

"Yes, ma'am. I'd do my damnedest to get my hand on the other side of your waistband. I'd slip the button, then slide down your zipper, real slow. And then I'd slip my hand down—"

CHAPTER 15

"Hello?" It was said softly. Kim's eyes widened and her blush deepened at the sound of Iris's voice. His sister, who'd entered with stealth into her own house. He stopped talking, and in a few moments, Iris appeared, in her stocking feet. Geoff behind her. The pair of them were creeping along like teenagers after curfew.

Both glanced at him and then stared at Kim. "How do you do that?" Geoff asked.

Kim smiled at him. "It's a gift. Babies like me. But I've also had lots of practice. You'll get there. You're their dad."

"I know, but they're so little and helpless. It's scary."

She smiled at both of them. "How was your evening?"

"It was wonderful," Iris said. "I can't tell you how nice it was to get out of this house, and talk to Geoff like an adult. I think I was losing my mind."

As she spoke, she lifted a pink-clad baby off of Kim's shoulder. She made a sound like an irritated kitten, then curled into Iris's neck. "But I missed them, too. James, what are you doing here? Did Mom send you to make sure I'm coping?"

"I brought a present from the yoga women. They dropped it off at the station." He repeated his mother's little white lie.

Which fooled Iris about as much as he'd guessed it would. "Sorry she put you up to checking on me."

"I wanted to see my niece and nephew anyway."

"And it was nice you could keep Kim company." From the way she glanced at him he wondered how much she'd heard of their baseball conversation.

"I'll help you put them to bed," Kim said, rising and resettling the other baby. The pair of them crept upstairs and in a few minutes, Kim returned alone.

"Iris is feeding them."

Geoff shook his head. "For such tiny little things, all they do is eat and poop."

"They'll grow bigger," Kim assured him. "Before you know it."

He nodded. "Thank you for tonight. Iris wouldn't trust anyone else."

"I was happy to look after them. Really, anytime."

He looked seriously grateful. "Thanks."

"I'll head out now. Tell Iris I'll call her tomorrow."

Before Geoff could invite him to stay, he said, "I only came to drop off that present. Tell Iris I'll call her tomorrow too."

"Sure thing."

He followed Kim down the hall and they both slipped on their shoes. He watched her blonde hair fall over her face, silky and rich. He wanted to run his hands through it. Watch it tangle as she tossed her head while he made love to her.

He said nothing until they were outside. The air was warming up. The evenings lasting longer.

"Well," she said, turning to him.

"It's not even ten. Do you want to go get some food or something?"

She stared at him. "I've only been in town for a couple of

months, but where exactly do you think you can find food at this time of night?"

James shook his head. "Sometimes I forget I'm not still in Seattle." He looked at her sheepishly. "I can cook you something. "

Her eyes widened. "You cook?"

"*Cook* might be too strong a term. Especially to a woman of your talent in the kitchen. Let me be more specific. I can barbecue a mean steak. Also grill a portobello mushroom for vegetarian sisters. And," he held up his finger as though inspiration had struck, "My grilled cheese sandwiches are world-famous."

"You know I start work at four in the morning."

He grimaced. "Right, I forgot. So, you probably need to get straight home."

She should, of course. If she had any self-preservation she would get into her car and point it for home. Jump in bed, pull the covers over her head and attempt not to think about him or how the baseball conversation had made her feel. But, she had already learned that around James she was not sensible.

She said, "Actually, I would love a sandwich. Babysitters usually get to raid the fridge, but I couldn't move with the babies."

"Understandable. So, it's really my civic duty to feed you, since you helped out my sister."

She shook her head at his foolishness. "I'll follow you in my car."

"When we've got more privacy, I'll finish explaining how baseball works."

"Now you're taking this to a whole new level." She teased him right back.

He came closer. Lowered his voice. "I'm thinking about sliding into home base."

"Phew. You're smooth."

"Come on, get in your car. You can follow me to my place."

"I don't have a toothbrush even."

"Quit stalling. I stocked up at Costco. I have eight tooth-brushes in assorted colors."

He walked her to her car, which she found adorable. He waited for her to unlock it and then opened the door for her and held it as she got in.

As she followed the lights of his truck back to his place, she knew she was heading into dangerous territory. And she couldn't do anything to stop herself.

"Now, I don't want you interfering in my kitchen," James ordered as she followed him with every intention of interfering.

She stopped. "I'm so sorry. I'm so used to cooking."

"Well forget it. In my kitchen I am boss." He pointed to the other side of the granite breakfast bar. "You can sit there and talk to me."

She leaned forward, her elbows on the counter, and watched him. He looked so hot, especially when he tied a kitchen towel around his waist, chef style, which she was pretty certain he'd done for her benefit. He pulled up his sleeves, washed his hands with as much fanfare as if he were a surgeon preparing to oper-ate, and then pulled out a loaf of bread. He fetched cheese and butter from the fridge and finally a jar of dill pickles.

He placed a serviceable looking skillet on the stovetop. This wasn't a pan he'd grabbed at a discount store. It was solid, heavy bottomed, and looked as though it had seen plenty of use. She'd be willing to bet there was more than grilled cheese sandwiches in this man's repertoire.

While the skillet heated he buttered both sides of the bread, sliced the cheese and placed generous slabs between the slices of bread. He put the first sandwich in the pan where it sizzled gently, suggesting he'd got the temperature exactly right.

As he prepared the second sandwich he said, "There are

plenty of people who add things to a grilled cheese: onions and avocado and ham, but for me, grilled cheese sandwich is best when it's simplest."

"I could not agree more. Sometimes the simple things are the best."

He pressed a spatula onto the cooking sandwich. "When we were kids, this was always the meal we had when we came in after hockey practice or a wet rugby game or swim team, when we were cold and hungry. Mom used to make it exactly this way."

The smell of the cooking sandwich made her mouth water watching. He reached for a knife, also high quality and well used, and sliced a dill pickle.

"Do you want something to drink with this?"

"What did you used to drink with it when you were kids?"

"Milk."

"A glass of milk would be nice."

Before she knew it, she had in front of her a perfectly cooked grilled cheese sandwich and three green pickle slices fanned out beside it.

She crunched into her sandwich and found it excellent. Crispy golden brown on the outside, and the cheese melted gooey on the inside.

"Oh this is so good."

He flipped his own sandwich onto a plate. "Did you have these as a kid?"

She shook her head. "Once in a while, if we went into town, we might get a hot dog. Mostly we ate what we grew ourselves and stocked up on the kind of supplies that last months."

"It doesn't sound like one of those back to the land dreamscapes."

"My dad did not want us mixing with other people and he was pretty paranoid now I think about it. We grew vegetables in the summer and ate a lot of potatoes and canned goods in the winter. Dried milk that you can reconstitute and never tasted like milk, you know? We raised chickens and made all our own bread and so on. I learned to cook mostly as a survival skill."

He nodded. "My folks raised chickens too, still do. And they grow vegetables, but my mom still went grocery shopping every week. With eleven kids, she had to. And a couple of us would get roped into going with her to help." He glanced at her with understanding. "You must have felt so lonely."

She nodded. Surprised he understood that it wasn't the hoeing potatoes, collecting eggs and shucking peas that had been hard. It was not having anyone her own age to play with.

She felt immediately uncomfortable telling him so much, so she jumped up to clean the kitchen but he waved her away. "My kitchen is my castle. Why don't you get ready for bed? Toothbrushes are in the bathroom cabinet."

She nodded. The last time they'd made love had been so spontaneous. There hadn't been the awkwardness of preparing for bed and picking a color toothbrush. What was she getting into? It was one thing to throw caution to the winds and enjoy crazy hot sex with a virtual stranger, but when they moved on to sleepovers and toothbrushes, well, they were moving into territory she wasn't completely comfortable with.

Still, she couldn't deny the pull of attraction that was keeping her here. She found her way to the bathroom. As he'd promised there was a jumbo pack of toothbrushes in a rainbow of colors. She chose a purple one. As she brushed her teeth, she noticed the shine of excitement in her eyes. His bathroom was as neat and orderly as though he were in the military. She supposed being a cop wasn't that far off. When she walked into his bedroom she halted in surprise. "Wow." She said aloud.

"What's the matter?"

"Nothing." She shook her head and simply regarded the bedroom. "Did you go on one of those home makeover shows?" His bedroom was masculine in the way that a female designer pictures masculine. The leather chair and ottoman in navy leather, with a tall stainless steel reading lamp beside it. A huge bed with a gray and black upholstered headboard. Luxury bedding in black, white and gray. A dark gray carpet so plush she longed to walk through it with bare feet. The art on the walls was of outdoor scenes, mostly photographs. Floor length drapes, in a fabric that complemented the bedspread hung in front of expensive-looking California shutters.

He strode forward and flipped on the fancy looking glass light on the fancy-looking bedside table. "No," he said, removing the coordinating cushions from the top of the bed. Efficiently he turned he slid back the duvet cover. "Worse than that. My sisters."

She grinned at the disgusted tone in his voice. "Not Iris?" Iris's home was nothing like this.

"Of course not. Iris is not a controlling fashion-obsessed autocrat who barges into other people's houses and dictates improvements."

She nodded slowly as understanding dawned. "Rose."

"Yep. With some help, I might add, from my twin Josh who said that with the gay gene he also got all the sense of style for both of us and so he owed it to me."

"Why didn't you tell them to mind their own business?"

"Rose tends to act first and ask permission later." He walked around the bed toward where she stood. "Plus, once you've slept in fancy Egyptian cotton sheets, you never want to go back. And that is a great reading chair. So, I made my peace with it."

"I think they did a great job."

He advanced slowly. "You are wearing way too many clothes. And I still have to finish my baseball lesson."

She giggled as he grabbed for her and in no time at all she was wearing no clothes at all. He undressed himself equally rapidly and then pulled her to him. When their bodies touched, she was lost.

CHAPTER 16

*S*he had barely fallen asleep, his arm curled around her possessively in a way that she found disturbingly comforting, when she was startled awake by the loud ringing of a telephone. Before she was fully conscious, James was reaching for his cell. "Sheriff Chance," he said, sitting up, throwing the duvet off his legs and climbing out of the bed in one efficient motion.

He listened for a moment and then sat back down on the bed, his spine curving away from her in irritation or defeat or perhaps a combination of both. "Loreen," he said, sounding exasperated. "It's almost midnight. What do you want?" He did not sound like a man ready to rush out to save the town. He sounded like a man with woman trouble.

He rubbed his eyes. "Yes, I know you have a kitten. If it's stuck on top of the fridge or up a tree or something it will have to wait for morning."

She could hear the tone on the other end of the phone more than words and they sounded hysterical.

And then he jumped to his feet once more. "What? Oh, damn it. You have got to be kidding me. Okay, okay, calm down. I'll be there as fast as I can. Just stay still and don't make any sudden movements."

More hysterical babbling.

"I know exactly how big that snake is. Whatever you do, don't get between it and the kitten. I'm on my way."

"What's going on?" She did not like that the conversation had included the words kitten and snake. She'd held the tiny ball of black and white fur and made it purr just by running a finger over its back.

He was already in his pants and reaching for his shirt. "Alice has escaped again. And she's got Loreen's kitten lined up as her next meal."

She jumped to her feet as well. "Oh, no."

"What are you doing?"

"I'm coming with you. Remember, I have snake wrangling experience. And it might take two of us to stop Alice from eating that kitten." She scrambled into her clothes.

As they strode out the door and into his truck, he made another call. "Lauren? I need you. Remember the picture I sent you of that snake? Yeah, the carpet python. It's escaped again." Briefly, he filled her in. "The owner said it only eats mice and small rodents. But she's at Loreen's place with that kitten you gave her. Will the snake try to eat the kitten?"

He sighed. "I was afraid of that. Thanks. I agree. We're on our way, but can you meet us at Loreen's?"

Then he handed Kim his cell. "Call Enid Parkinson and tell her to get her ass to Loreen's."

There was no traffic on the road, so he drove at top speed. When they arrived at one of the nicer houses in the newer part of town he ran to the door, Kim racing to keep up. The door opened before he got there. Loreen was fully dressed and fully made up. She wore tight jeans and a black, cashmere sweater with a low, scooped neck.

"Thank God you're here. I don't know what to do. Poor

Snuffy is absolutely terrified." She slapped a perfectly-manicured hand to her chest. "And so am I."

James nodded. "Where is Snuffy at the moment?"

He didn't blink at the stupid name, but treated the matter of a terrified kitten seriously. She thought that was a nice quality in a small-town sheriff.

"She climbed up the bedroom room curtains. But she's so little I'm scared she'll fall. That horrible snake is trying to get her."

"Right."

He strode to the bedroom and Kimberly tried not to wonder how he knew exactly where it was. There had to be a bunch of perfectly good reasons for that. None of which included Loreen and James in any kind of intimate situations similar to, say, the one that she and James had just been in.

She followed him into Loreen's bedroom.

The tiny, clearly-terrified kitten had managed to scramble from the curtain onto a tall bureau where it stood with its paws straight out and its back arched, its fur on end, looking as though it had been electrocuted. It was hissing, but feebly because it was only a baby.

The snake had managed to climb up onto the bed. Its cold gaze was fixed on its prey, and its tongue flicked in and out as though it were licking its lips. James moved so fast she never saw it coming. He reached out and grabbed the snake, picking it up and holding it away from his body. If a snake could make facial expressions, this one looked pretty mad.

She ran forward and scooped up the kitten which, too agitated to realize she was friend and not foe, hissed some more and scratched at her hands. "Shh, it's okay." She passed the kitten to Loreen.

"Oh, my poor, poor, baby," Loreen cooed. Snuffy made a small mewing sound and snuggled into her sweater.

Loreen stared at them with big, scared eyes. "Now what do we do?"

"Kim, there's a burlap sack in the back of my truck. Can you get it?"

"Sure."

"But what if it bites you, James? Is it poisonous?" Loreen wanted to know.

"No. It's only dangerous to small rodents."

"That's a relief. I almost had a heart attack I was so scared."

Kim was almost at the front door when someone knocked. She opened the door and Lauren came in carrying a burlap sack and a cage.

Lauren took in the situation at a glance. Her eyes widened slightly when she saw Kim, and softened in relief when she spied the kitten. And then she said, "Where's Alice?"

"In Loreen's bedroom, with James."

"Oh, my God. What kind of lunatic keeps a kitten-murdering snake as a pet? And calls it Alice?"

James came out, holding Alice. "Nice work, bro," Lauren said. She took the snake from him, and he held the portable cage while she eased Alice into it.

Snuffy seemed to have recovered somewhat from its fright and was purring against the cashmere sweater.

A more timid knock fell on the door and this time it was Alice's owner. The woman looked sheepish and a little frightened. "Oh, Sheriff Chance. I'm so sorry. I don't know why Alice is being so troublesome."

Loreen turned to the older woman and snapped. "I want that snake destroyed. It terrorized me, and invaded my property and almost killed my baby."

KIM FELT that Loreen really wanted someone to lash out at, since she'd had such a scare. It seemed James did too. He said, "Miss Parkinson, I am going to have to give you a ticket. And we need to get Alice secured properly so she doesn't terrorize the people of Hidden Falls any more."

Enid nodded her head humbly. "I'll do anything you ask, please don't take away my baby." A tear rolled down her wrinkled cheek as she went closer and peered at Alice inside the cage. "Please don't hurt her."

James said, "My sister Lauren's a veterinarian."

"Is Alice all right?" Enid asked.

"Is the snake fine? What about me? It was on my bed!"

"I'll pay to have the bedspread cleaned. It's the least I can do."

"You bet your ass it is," Loreen said.

"Good," said James. "I'm going to suggest that Lauren comes by and assesses Alice's living conditions. Maybe she can help you make sure she doesn't escape again. That's what you really want, isn't it Loreen?"

She nodded, seeing the older woman's tears. "There's no harm done. So long as I never see that hideous snake again."

Lauren and Enid Parkinson left together.

As she and James were about to follow, Loreen said, "So, are you two an item?"

She froze. She'd never thought of the obvious implication when she was seen in public at midnight with James, both of them obviously fresh out of bed. She struggled for an excuse that might have involved a police emergency at the bakery when, to her surprise, he said, "Yes. We are."

She felt such a whirlwind of emotion she didn't know which was more prominent. The thrill of hearing those words, the wishing they were true, the yearning to be with James, the sadness of knowing it could never be. By the time they got into his truck and he'd started up the engine and was backing out, she burst out with, "I am so sorry!"

He paused in the backup process and turned his head to regard her. "Sorry about what?"

"That I put you in that position. I should have stayed away."

He looked at her and then a crease appeared between his eyebrows. "Does it bother you that I said we were an item?"

"Yes." It bothered her so much she couldn't stand it. She wanted him and couldn't have him. And now Loreen would tell everyone the gossip about the Sheriff and the bakery assistant and she'd have to deal with raised eyebrows and whispers behind her back.

"I said that to keep Loreen away from me. Since you work at gossip central you must know that she's been, um, interested."

"Oh. Okay."

"But I do want us to be an item. I'm crazy about you. Is that a problem?"

"We both know it's a problem." She felt as though a huge weight were pressing on her chest. "I should have left when you confronted me about my family."

He changed gears with a jerk. "Maybe you should have."

CHAPTER 17

*H*e drove home in silence, and it felt like a heavy silence. She followed him into his house and he said, "Do you want a drink?"

"A drink? It's after one. I have to get up in a couple of hours."

He looked as though he wanted to argue, but merely nodded. "Come on. I'll tuck you in."

"No. I need to go." From being one of the best evenings of her life this was fast turning into one of the worst.

She grabbed her bag. He stopped her before she got to the door. "Am I going too fast?" he asked her, looking both hurt and confused, and so seriously delectable that she wanted to drag him back into his bedroom and take things even faster.

But she couldn't. She shook her head sadly, "Too complicated."

He looked as frustrated as she felt. "Okay, so your dad deals drugs. I hate that he does. But he's in a different country. Not my jurisdiction."

"But if he gets busted, and finds out I'm seeing a cop? He'll blame me."

"He should blame himself for breaking the law and spreading

misery and addiction." His words were terse, his eyes the color of steel.

"What if they needed evidence to convict? How do I know you wouldn't try and convince me?"

"I guess you'd have to trust me."

She gnawed her lip. "My mom, my siblings, if any of them thought I'd betrayed Dad I'd lose them. Don't you see?"

And the way he looked at her and nodded, she could see that he did.

She barely slept for what was left of the night and when she did it was to have one of those dreams where a dark force was chasing her and she couldn't run fast enough. She woke with her heart pounding and a feeling of disorientation, then reality reasserted itself. She knew exactly where she was and how foolish she'd been.

She rehearsed a cool and professional morning greeting for James when he came into Sunflower, but all her rehearsals and orders to her cheeks not to blush were wasted.

James didn't come in.

Not in the morning.

Not for lunch.

Not for an afternoon coffee.

Not once.

As she locked up, she felt the grittiness of fatigue behind her eyelids and the drag of sadness. She'd planned to stop by Iris's house on her way home as she did most days but she didn't have the energy for Iris's kind eyes that missed nothing. Iris also had a quality about her that made a person want to unload their troubles. Since she was also James's sister, she was the worst person for Kim to unload on. Besides, Kim never shared her troubles. She'd learned long ago to keep her head down and her mouth shut. Never get involved.

Until she came to this crazy town and somehow got tangled up with the Chances, that attitude had kept everybody she cared about safe. Now she'd gone and fallen for the sheriff, of all people, and love had made her crazy.

She heard the jangle of the Sunflower door chimes as she shut the door with more force than necessary, like someone laughing at her from inside the door.

Love?

Where had that word even come from?

She didn't love James. He was a distraction, a gorgeous, kind, funny, strong, decent man who made her weak at the knees, but she didn't love him.

Did she?

She'd never felt this way in her life. As she thought about moving on, never seeing James again, that familiar heaviness pressed on her chest. Oh, no. This feeling, this up and down, happy and sad, wanting to see him all the time, thinking about him, wondering what he was doing. Wanting to see that special expression in his eyes when he looked at her.

That wasn't love, was it?

As she trudged to her car she had to accept the horrifying possibility that she, Kimberly Parker, whose father was a drug dealer, was in love with the sheriff.

Her shoulders hunched. There was no one around to hear her one word acknowledgement of finding herself in love for the first time in her life.

"Crap!"

TOO COMPLICATED? What the hell was wrong with the woman? James couldn't stop thinking about the way Kim had looked at him with big, guilty eyes as she was heading out of his door and told him being with him was too complicated.

What was complicated about two people who liked each other

spending time together? What was complicated about two people who liked each other *and had blisteringly good sex* spending time together?

When he thought of the all-too brief time they'd spent in his bed, which he did far too often for a man with a jurisdiction to protect, he thought the sex was more than just physical. Made him feel like a fool to even think that way, but when they'd been naked and entwined together, moving as though they were dancing to the perfect melody, they'd shared more than skin to skin contact and earth-shattering climaxes. He felt that he'd reached her on a much deeper level.

You couldn't hold a woman while she trembled in ecstasy, looking into her eyes, and not see into her deepest places. Most women he'd slept with closed their eyes or turned inward when they climaxed, but not Kim. She'd held his gaze with her own and he'd watched as her lips trembled on a cry, as her body had quaked and spasmed around his. Her eyes had grown brighter so he was reminded of stars, and, as his own climax started, he hadn't been able to turn his gaze away, either, opening himself to her completely, letting her see everything he was and had been and ever would be.

At least, that's how it had felt at the time. Now all he felt was a fool. He'd fallen for a woman who'd been skittish from the start. She'd looked so pretty and waif-like, so lost somehow that the need to protect had made him want to slay her dragons and ride her home on his white charger.

But the dragon was her own father. What would Kim do to protect her dad, even though he was on the wrong side of the law?

He wondered if she'd even stay around long enough for Iris to get back on her feet, or whether she'd pack her old heap of a car and hit the road one night, with nothing but the moon to guide her. If he saw her driving away, he half hoped he'd have the strength not to try and stop her.

One thing he could do was not spook her anymore, for Iris's sake and that of his tiny niece and nephew. So, he drank the station coffee, and that was a sacrifice in itself. Instead of steaming fresh morning glory muffins, he hit the Old Mill diner and ate pancakes. Just wasn't the same. Somehow, not following his usual morning routine with a stop at Sunflower threw off his whole day. He felt like he wasn't quite firing on all cylinders.

July 4th was only a few days away so he drove to the fairground where the battle re-enactors were practicing. Sure enough, he found a straggling bunch of mostly old guys parading around with guns. One old boy gamely shouldered his musket, then moved his walker along a foot or two, then had to readjust his rifle. He was slightly concerned to see what looked like a black canon on wheels. He hadn't reckoned on field artillery.

He was about to head closer and take a look when his radio sounded. Connie said, "I need to take my lunch hour and the deputy's off somewhere. He's not answering. You coming in or should I lock up?"

Hidden Falls' Sheriff's Office might not be the most advanced law enforcement operation in the country but he drew the line at locking up the place over lunch hour. Instead of heading down to see what was going on with the reenactment group, he said, "I'm on my way. Give me five minutes," and headed back to the station.

JULY in the Pacific Northwest could be as rainy as November, and frequently was, but this year, July the fourth dawned sunny with not so much as a wisp of cloud in the sky. As James headed to the fairground, he tried not to think about how good a Sunflower coffee would taste right now. It was going to be a long day and the coffee he'd brewed himself hadn't set him up the way Sunflower coffee did, especially when he added a couple of muffins.

But he was sticking to his guns. If Kim thought being with him was too complicated then he'd leave her be.

He was on hand to see the end of the 5K race, happy to see Geoff in the top ten finishers. The pancake breakfast, under Daphne's direction, was running smoothly. He accepted a plate of pancakes and joined a table, making small talk with his community.

He had half of his attention on the day and half on Kim. He'd never, ever been the kind of man to pester a woman who'd turned him down.

The fact that Kim had turned him down after some of the best sex of his life definitely soured his mood. If they'd never become intimate he could put the entire incident down to unrequited lust. It happened. Not all that often, if he was honest with himself. Usually, in his life, when he'd felt lust it had been returned. With interest.

And Kim could throw up her hands and cry 'complicated' as much as she liked, but he'd been in that bed with her and experienced the almost magical connection between them and he knew she'd felt it too. Sex, the first time with someone new, was almost always a little awkward as each partner felt their way around the other.

He tried to make any woman who was kind enough to share his bed feel special, to put her pleasure first. He was fairly certain that he'd succeeded at least most of the time. But with Kim he hadn't even had to work at it. The natural way they'd moved together, the unspoken connection, the held gazes, the explosive climaxes, that had been a whole new level of pleasure. If they'd been that good their first couple of times out, he couldn't imagine how great they'd be together with a bit of practice.

Well, yes, he could. He had thought of little else since the sexiest baker he'd ever met had walked away from him.

Maybe, on some level, he was hoping that if he left her alone, she'd come to him. So far that hadn't happened.

Why couldn't her dad have chosen to be a plumber, a bricklayer, a fireman, an astronaut, any one of a thousand professions that would leave Kim free to love him? To trust him.

Loreen had taken her duties as media liaison seriously, he saw. Not only was a photographer from the Hidden Falls Gazette shooting pictures, but she had a cameraman from the local news station following her as she interviewed some of the runners and a family happily munching on pancakes.

His deputy was walking around the kids' attractions so James decided to stroll over to where the battle re-enactment would take place in the big field behind the fair.

As he got closer, he heard the drums.

War drums.

CHAPTER 18

When he'd idly watched the practice of the reenactment, there had only been Wilfred Ohmerson banging the drum. Wilfred was a high school senior who went to marching band camp every summer. But there was more than one drum banging away as he strode up. As he hit the rise he had a full view over the battlefield, and he saw what could have been a scene from a historical TV series about the Revolutionary War, if you deducted a few decades off most of the reenactors. He was impressed at the level of detail in the costumes, the props, and most of all the guns.

He walked down the hill to find Harold offering a demonstration of how to load and shoot a flintlock. A small crowd had already gathered and he could see that Harold was in his element. He was dressed as a general. No surprise there. He doubted that George Washington himself had looked as good.

As he grew closer, he could hear the words. "British had the Brown Bess. Later in the war the French supplied the Charleville musket. It's a front loader with a range of a hundred and fifty yards."

He could see that a few gun enthusiasts and young boys were

hanging on every word. "The musket weighs fourteen pounds." Harold hefted it a few times, "Then you add in five pounds of ammunition plus gun powder, it gets pretty heavy."

"What's the fastest you can load a musket?" asked a boy in the crowd.

Harold lit up at the question. "I don't know," he said. "Let's find out. Have you got a stop watch?"

The kid looked at him like he really was more than two hundred and fifty years old. "Yeah. On my phone."

"Right. Of course. Well, you say 'Go,' and then time me."

The kid pressed a couple of buttons then nodded. "Go," he said, and pressed start.

Harold grabbed a paper cone from his leather pouch, tore it open with his teeth, and followed all the instructions he'd given them earlier. James had to hand it to him, he really was pretty fast. When he drew the gun to the firing position, he commanded, "Stop." Then to the kid, "How long?"

"Twenty-seven seconds."

Harold shook his head. "A good rifleman can do it faster. Let's go again."

He placed the rifle beside him, leaning against a rail where a series of muskets were stored, and grabbed a second musket. "Okay, tell me when."

This time, his record was nineteen seconds. He nodded as his small audience clapped and continued to answer questions.

He pulled out a period-perfect pocket watch. "Now, if you'll excuse me, I have to go to war."

The group clapped and then followed him as he strode purposefully to where the two sides were setting up for battle.

James wished he could rid himself of the feeling of unease that gripped him. He'd watched footage of other re-enactments and knew that the black powder would go 'bang' but without a musket ball there was no danger of anyone getting hurt. He was more worried about heart attacks and strokes and had made sure that the first aid van was close by.

The red and blue coats were as bright as children's toys, and the buff pantaloons gleamed in the sun so James reached for his sunglasses. The faces of the warriors were earnest and eager. These were not battle-hardened campaigners. They were accountants and dentists, desk jockeys, bored retirees and young men who looked as though they'd never had a date. The drummers rehearsed beside a rest station with lawn chairs and a big blue plastic cooler.

His eyes scanned the area and he spotted Loreen and her cameraman setting up. Charlie, the mayor, thought the reenactment was such a good idea that he'd asked for extra footage for the town's archives.

As James watched, orders were shouted, drummers drummed, the chairs and coolers were pushed behind a stand of trees and suddenly he felt like he was watching a PBS documentary. The two sides lined up, closer than he'd imagined opposing armies would, but of course the old muskets wouldn't have much of a firing range.

He'd been briefed about what would happen. The riflemen would pack only a small amount of gunpowder into the muzzles, not the lead musket balls that would make the antique flintlocks dangerous. The gunpowder would flash and bang and emit a puff of smoke. The redcoats would pretend to be routed and the crowd would cheer.

The spectators were staying at a safe range as they'd been instructed. Harold was at the head of his army. An unknown player from Ohio led the Brits. He had to hand it to Harold. The turnout was the best they'd had in years.

Soldiers moved into formation. These guys had obviously been practicing. They pulled paper cones from leather pouches, as he'd seen Harold do in his demonstration. They tore them open with their teeth, poured black powder into the muzzles of their flintlocks, detached the ramrods and pounded the powder into the barrels, then they cocked the muskets. The first line of Brits fell to its knees and assumed the firing position. There was a moment of utter silence as everyone waited for the order to fire.

One older man to Harold's left was still fumbling with his gun and it took James a minute to comprehend why. "No!" he yelled, already moving toward the battle lines.

The older gentleman seemed to be under the impression he was in an actual battle and the thing he was fumbling with was a paper wrapped object about the size of a marble. He could be going for the ultimate in verisimilitude, pushing a fake ball into the barrel of his musket along with gunpowder; or the old crackpot was going to murder a guy who woke up this morning thinking he was going to play at soldiers and could well end the day six feet under.

James was running before he'd finished the thought. "Stop!" he yelled, his feet hurdling over the lumpy grass, his arms windmilling. "Stop!"

In the heat of battle, no one heard him. He crashed through the gaggle of spectators, threw himself between the the two lines. The red and blue blurred in his peripheral vision. He yelled, "Hold your—"

"Fire!" commanded Harold.

He could see the old guy's rifle aimed at a young man with troubling acne. As guns began to explode all around him, sending puffs of acrid smoke into the air, he threw himself at the clueless fake British soldier. The kid yelped as he knocked into him and they both went flying, along with an authentic Brown Bess, smoke trailing from it like a doomed aircraft. The airborne nanosecond during which James thought he'd made a complete fool of himself was followed by a moment of pure agony as he felt the impact of the musket ball tearing through his flesh.

With a roar he fell to the ground. For minutes he was aware of nothing but searing pain, people running, staring faces, a man dressed in regimentals saying in a voice as crisp as a starched bed sheet, "Back up, please, I'm a GP."

"Is he dead?"

And then Loreen's cameraman, from much too close. "Thank God, we got it all on video!"

The doctor made a swift, painful examination. He glanced up and saw his mom looking frantic. "James. Are you all right?"

The doctor said, "He's very lucky. The ball grazed his gluteus maximus and he's—"

Loreen Ludlow held out a microphone. He felt the huge eye of the camera staring at him in his most humiliating moment. "Gluteus maximus? Are you saying the sheriff got shot in the butt?"

His ass was on fire, and James thought the pain from this day had just begun.

CHAPTER 19

$\mathcal{K}$im was ready to roll. She'd moved so many times that she could pack her little car with absolute efficiency. Not an inch of wasted space. She gazed at it sadly. All her worldly possessions fit neatly into a decade old hatchback.

But this was the first time she'd dreaded leaving. Because this time she wasn't taking all her possessions with her when she left. She'd be leaving her heart behind.

She'd chosen today to leave so she could slip out of town while everyone was celebrating July 4th at the fairground.

How many times was she going to do this? Pack up and disappear? Move on? Her whole life had been dictated by her father's rules. No going into town. Homeschooling. Only socializing with the rest of the cartel as she'd taken to calling them. Chores. Learning to stitch wounds and birth babies. And most of all, No Cops.

She'd never rebelled. She'd escaped. Her dad had been furious, but no terrible consequences had ensued. She knew she could go home any time she wanted and her family would welcome her back with open arms. And a list of jobs her mom couldn't get to.

She was sick and tired of running away. She wanted to love

James, freely and happily. She wanted to make a home. To put down roots. To stay. Maybe she'd like to be able to adopt a stray kitten, have kids one day.

She stared at her packed car one more time, then, firming her jaw, she took out her cell phone and called her parents. Her mom answered. "Kimi, it's so good to hear from you. Is everything all right?"

"I think it will be. But I need to talk to Dad."

"Are you sure, honey? You don't want to talk to me first?" She'd always gone through her mother, who'd act as go between. But Kim felt that it was time she stood on her own two feet. In fact, it was way past time.

"I'm sure, Mom."

"Okay." And she yelled for Kim's dad. She could hear them in the background. Her dad: *What does she want?* Her mom: *I don't know. She wouldn't say.* Then a *hmmmph* and her dad was on the phone. "Kim, sweetheart, when are you coming home?"

She felt sick in her stomach, so shaky she had to sit down in the passenger seat of her car. She was a grown woman and she was still frightened of her father's disapproval. She pulled in a breath and knew this was a moment that would define her future, however it played out. She said, "Dad, I'm in love with a wonderful man." Oh, that wasn't what she'd planned to say first. She was messing up already.

"Who is he?" her father asked. He sounded wary and she knew right away that he was more concerned about how Kim's new man would affect him than he was about his daughter's happiness. She began to feel angry which at least lessened the butterflies in her stomach.

"His name is James Chance. And he's the Sheriff of Hidden Falls, Oregon. The town I live in."

She didn't have to wait long for the explosion. "Did you say Sheriff? What the Hell, Kimi. Why don't you come on up here with handcuffs right now and slap your old man in jail. Then where will you and your mom and your brothers and sisters be? Where's the loyalty?" He was yelling, louder and louder, working himself up into a rage.

She trembled because she always trembled when he got angry, but she was tired of backing down. She waited until he took a breath and then she said, "Dad, I want you to retire."

"Retire?" He yelled the word so loud she had to pull the phone away from her ear. Far away.

"Yes. You don't need the money. Our whole family has lived in fear ever since I can remember. You've been lucky. You've never been convicted. Why don't you quit while you're ahead? Go fishing. Enjoy life."

"Since when do you make the decisions around here?" he bellowed, but he hadn't hung up so she took hope from that.

"I don't," she said quietly. "But I need to start making my own decisions in life. I've always played by your rules. Done everything you've asked of me. Now, I'm asking you to do something for me. I love you and Mom and the kids and I swear I'd never do anything to hurt you. But I love this man and I think I have a real shot at happiness. Like you and Mom have. Don't you want that for me?"

She heard him breathing and she kept quiet. Then he said, "You bring any sonofabitch cop near my place and I'll shoot him. You got that?"

"Yes, Daddy."

He huffed some more. "And don't think I'm coming to your wedding."

Since he couldn't cross the border it had never occurred to her that he would. Not that she was thinking marriage.

Yet.

"But Mom could come, right?"

"Don't you get ahead of yourself. He going to use you to get to me?"

"He says he won't. But I would hate to have my father and the man I love on opposite sides of the law. So, I'm asking you, please, please, retire."

"You've got some nerve!"

She laughed shakily. "Honestly, it took all my courage to phone you."

"Well, I'm not saying yes. I'll think about it."

She knew she'd got much more than she could have hoped. "Thank you, Daddy."

"Here's your mother."

A second later her mom was on the phone. "Oh, Baby, I'm so excited for you. Are you really getting married?"

"I don't know. Maybe. Will you come?"

"If I can." Then, "Oh, the hell with it. Yes. I'm coming. And if that man decides he doesn't want me back, then he can do his own cooking and mending and weeding."

"I love you, Mom."

"I love you, too, Kimi. I've got to go calm your father down now, but let's talk next week and you can tell me all about your new man."

"I will."

It was a while before she could get her legs to work well enough to drive. She should unpack her stuff, but she really, really needed to see James first. To tell him the good news.

Wiping a tear from her cheek, she headed for the fairgrounds.

When she arrived, she jogged straight for the largest crowd, assuming that's where she'd find the sheriff. She couldn't wait one more minute to tell him her news. She'd finally stood up for herself to her father. And it hadn't been terrible. In fact, she had a feeling he was glad of an excuse to get out of the business. At least she hoped so.

But whatever happened, she'd made her choice and she was staying. She only hoped James still wanted her as much as she wanted him.

She was huffing, out of breath when she grew closer. A lot of men in period costume were mingling with the crowd who were gathered around a central spot. Her heart clutched as she took in the scene, saw the lights on in the first aid van, and realized someone was hurt.

"What's going on?" she asked a tall man who looked as though he could see over the knot of people.

"Sheriff's been shot," he said.

"What?" She screamed the word and began pushing and shoving her way forward. "Let me through!" As she got close enough to see what was going on her worst fears were allayed.

James wasn't dead. He was lying on his side on the ground looking pale. An old man in a Revolutionary uniform was mumbling, "I'm sorry, James. I usually shoot at a target. Forgot I wasn't supposed to use a ball. I'm real sorry."

Daphne was sitting beside James, along with Lauren and Cooper. Geoff was standing a foot away. There were people she knew from the coffee shop and others she recognized from around town. But the person who most alarmed her was Loreen Ludlow, standing near to James with a camera pointed at her.

"James, what happened!" she cried, throwing herself on her knees beside him.

"Accident," he said. He sounded irate which she assumed was the pain and the fact that he was crowded around by spectators.

"He got shot in the butt!" Cooper announced, barely containing a snort of laughter.

Lauren snapped, "Shut up, Cooper. He saved a man's life!"

"Oh, James, I'm so sorry."

But he was looking at her as though she might be a hallucination. "What are you doing here? Thought you were leaving. Cooper said he saw you packing your car when he drove by."

"I've got so much to tell you, but later. I'm staying."

He looked as though he wasn't sure this was good news. "Why?"

She took a deep breath. She felt that way too many people

were listening, and a news camera was filming, but now that she'd started being brave she liked the feeling. "Because I love you!"

He smiled at her. She loved the way his eyes crinkled at the corners. "That is very good news." He reached for her and she leaned down to kiss him, a kiss full of promise. "I love you, too."

"What can I do?" she asked.

"Promise you'll still love me when I'm a national joke," he replied.

"What?"

"Loreen. She's getting patched in to the network so she can report live about the sheriff who got shot in the ass."

She recalled the family party where he'd admitted that his greatest fear was being shot in the butt and the humiliation it would cause. And once more her new found bravery asserted itself. "Give me a minute." She rose to her feet.

Loreen was fussing with her hair. "Are we ready to go?" she asked the cameraman.

"We'll be live in two minutes."

"Excellent."

"Loreen!" Kim said, speaking loud enough that everyone around could hear. "James saved a life today. That's the story. Where he was shot has nothing to do with it."

She received a thin smile from Loreen. "Honey, you bake great cookies, but let me decide what's news."

The cameraman laughed. "A sheriff getting shot in the butt! That'll be on every network in the country. Might even go international."

She was so mad she was vibrating.

"One minute," the camera guy warned.

She had one minute. Sixty seconds. She had to make them count. "Loreen, if you dare say one word about where Sheriff Chance was shot, I will make sure you are never served in Sunflower again." As a threat it wasn't much but it was all she could think of. Loreen loved her skinny lattes and came in at least once a day for what she called her fix. Usually twice.

She rolled her eyes. "Please, you're the hired help."

Geoff stepped forward. "She's right. I know my wife. You won't get served. You either," he said, gesturing to the guy with the camera.

A new voice joined in. "And I'll make sure no vet will treat your kitten." It was Lauren speaking. She stepped forward beside Kim. Now there were three of them lined up. Kim barely knew Lauren but she was positive that was a bluff. Lauren loved animals.

Still, Loreen began to look alarmed. "This is news. You can't stop me reporting news!"

"Thirty seconds."

Daphne joined them. "I'm sorry, Loreen, but you won't be welcome in Yoga or book club any more if you do this."

"What?" She glanced around. "You're going to shun me?" She caught sight of Charlie Mars, the mayor. "Charlie, are you going to let that happen?"

He said, "We all like and respect Sheriff Chance. You embarrass him and I'm going to make sure you never get access to me, my council, or the press bulletins we send out."

"Fifteen seconds."

Kim grabbed the young man whose life James had saved. He looked shaken, and very young in his British uniform. She said, "You need to go on camera and tell this reporter what happened today. Can you do that?"

He nodded. Gulped. "Guy saved my life. Least I can do."

She pulled him toward Loreen. "Here's your story." And pushed the blushing young man forward. Cooper joined the line of Chances, a human wall that protected James from the prying eye of the camera.

"And we're live," the cameraman said.

Loreen put on a professional smile and said, "I'm standing in

Hidden Falls, where a July 4th celebration almost turned deadly. Thanks to the heroic actions of the town's sheriff…"

"QUIET EVERYBODY, IT'S ON," Daphne announced, turning the volume up on the TV.

James was stretched out on the sofa. On his side. The emergency doc had told him he was lucky. The wound was clean and only needed four stitches. He was home, resting, but one by one his family had all dropped by with gifts and cards and well wishes. Cooper brought cold beer, which James happily tucked into. Kim sat on the floor with her hand in James's. She couldn't stand to be apart from him, having so nearly lost him.

Now was the moment of truth. The item had made the six o'clock news. What would Loreen do? Would she dare the entire community and go with the story that humiliated James? Or would she treat the story with the dignity that Kim felt it deserved?

While the news anchor did the lead in, James leaned forward and whispered, "I love you."

She put her lips to his ear and said, "I love you, too." Now they'd started they couldn't stop saying the words and she suspected they both realized how close they'd come to losing each other. If that musket ball had hit higher—she couldn't complete the thought. Instead she held James's hand and wished she never had to let it go.

There was Loreen, interviewing Gary Parks, the young man who'd almost died. There was footage of the re-enactment, and of James running, running, and the bang of the muskets and him knocking Gary out of the way. Loreen described the sequence of events and ended by saying, "Sheriff James Chance was shot in…" Everyone in James's living room held their breath until she finished the sentence "…the line of duty."

The laughter that erupted was so loud she couldn't hear the rest of the report, but she saw the Mayor being interviewed and knew he was saying what a hero James was, and then Harold came on, looking pale and shaken. And finally, Daphne shushed them all and Loreen was saying, "We've been told that at Sheriff Chance's request, no one will be charged in this near-tragic accident."

The anchor wanted to know if the shot officer was all right and Loreen assured him that his injuries were not life threatening.

"Except that he won't sit down for a week!" Cooper shouted to the TV.

James threw a cushion at him. "Kiss my line of duty!"

The Sheriff's Sweet Surrender - Book 6

The Daisy Game - Book 7

Chance Encounter - Prequel

Take a Chance Box Set - Prequel and Books 1-3

Nancy Warren Mystery

Vampire Knitting Club

Tangles and Treasons - a free prequel for Nancy's newsletter subscribers

The Vampire Knitting Club - Book 1

Stitches and Witches - Book 2

Crochet and Cauldrons - Book 3

Stockings and Spells - Book 4

Purls and Potions - Book 5

Fair Isle and Fortunes - Book 6

Lace and Lies - Book 7

Bobbles and Broomsticks - Book 8

Popcorn and Poltergeists - Book 9

Garters and Gargoyles - Book 10

Diamonds and Daggers - Book 11

Cat's Paws and Curses a Holiday Whodunnit

Vampire Knitting Club Boxed Set 1-3

The Vampire Knitting Club Boxed Set 4-6

The Vampire Book Club

A middle aged witch gets sent to Ireland to run an unusual book shop.

The Vampire Book Club - Book 1

Chapter and Curse - Book 2

A Spelling Mistake - Book 3

The Great Witches Baking Show

The Great Witches Baking Show - Book 1

Baker's Coven - Book 2

A Rolling Scone - Book 3

A Bundt Instrument - Book 4

Blood, Sweat and Tiers - Book 5

Toni Diamond Mysteries

Toni is a successful saleswoman for Lady Bianca Cosmetics in this series of humorous cozy mysteries. Along with having an eye for beauty and a head for business, Toni's got a nose for trouble and she's never shy about following her instincts, even when they lead to murder.

Frosted Shadow - Book 1

Ultimate Concealer - Book 2

Midnight Shimmer - Book 3

A Diamond Choker For Christmas - A Toni Diamond Mysteries Novella

For a complete list of books, check out Nancy's website at nancywarren.net

ABOUT THE AUTHOR

Nancy Warren is the USA Today Bestselling author of more than 70 novels. She's originally from Vancouver, Canada, though she tends to wander and has lived in England, Italy and California at various times. Favorite moments include being the answer to a crossword puzzle clue in Canada's National Post newspaper, being featured on the front page of the New York Times when her book Speed Dating launched Harlequin's NASCAR series, and being nominated three times for Romance Writers of America's RITA award. She has an MA in Creative Writing from Bath Spa University. She's an avid hiker, loves chocolate and most of all, loves to hear from readers! The best way to stay in touch is to sign up for Nancy's newsletter at www.nancywarren.net or her Facebook group www.facebook.com/groups/NancyWarren-Knitwits

To learn more about Nancy and her books
www.nancywarren.net

www.ingramcontent.com/pod-product-compliance
Lightning Source LLC
Chambersburg PA
CBHW061237170626
46809CB00007B/2713